A FICKLE MIND

ALEX NORONHA

© Alexe Noronha 2022

All rights reserved

All rights reserved by author. No part of this publication may be reproduced, stored in a retrieval system or transmitted in any form or by any means, electronic, mechanical, photocopying, recording or otherwise, without the prior permission of the author.

Although every precaution has been taken to verify the accuracy of the information contained herein, the author and publisher assume no responsibility for any errors or omissions. No liability is assumed for damages that may result from the use of information contained within.

First Published in February 2022

ISBN: 978-93-93388-81-0

Price: INR 238

BLUEROSE PUBLISHERS

www.bluerosepublishers.com
info@bluerosepublishers.com
+91 8882 898 898

Cover Design:
Akash Bartwal

Typographic Design:
Ilma Mirza

Distributed by: BlueRose, Amazon, Flipkart

Author Introduction

Alex Noronha is an upcoming writer, and this is his second book. His first book "Foolhardy" was an excellent thrilling experience and he continuous to keep it up with his second creation. A working professional with an eye to notice minute things captures events in his book that relates with our daily life but with a breath-taking climax

A pleasant Sunday afternoon at a local food outlet in Palolem, Goa was suddenly turned into a biker's fiesta. The firing from these bikes echoed around the place like guns firing in the battlefield. Fifteen bikers halted here to grab a bite. Immediately they caught attention of people in and around the restaurant. They all got down from their bike and waited for their leader to take charge. There were many such biker gangs across Goa but this one was different, and the difference was their leader. The leader of this gang was a fearless beautiful girl in her twenties. She was famous for her red jacket and a tattoo of a book on the left side of her neck. Her unique red jacket and that uncommon tattoo for a biker became her identity. Her name was Sara, and she was an orphan who stayed alone at an isolated place and lived her life in the moment. She was also a private investigator which was her only source of income. With time she solved many cases and rose to fame. She hired people to unload some of her work, and few helped her voluntarily. As time passed, her group turned into a Posse. They called themselves "Saviours".

Saviours were very often seen bringing justice in and around Goa. They helped the local cops in making Goa a peaceful place and they did it by staying within their legal rights.

Table for them was set up at the backyard and Sara managed the show. Today wasn't just a normal lunch for the Saviours, today they were all set out on a mission, a mission to find a thief who had created menace around Goa by robbing the churches and was labelled "Godless" by the people.

The unique thing about this thief was that he only robbed churches, and this made the locals extremely furious. As per the news, so far, he had stolen from twenty churches. But people believed that the numbers could easily be on the higher side and the money stolen was more than what was reported on the news. Nobody had any clue who Godless was, not the priest, not the people and certainly not the cops. He was never spotted by anyone anywhere and was like a ghost. He was also smart like a fox and never left any clue which made it impossible for the cops to track him.

His ways of stealing made him famous. For some people he was like James Bond, always a step ahead of the cops. People admired him for his smartness and among so many of his admirer was Sara. It was a surprise how a private investigator hired to catch the thief, admired the thief. But this admiration towards Godless was a secret crush and nobody knew about it. Sara was concerned about how it played games with her mind, but she was still focused on catching him, no matter what. Local news made Godless a hero and she had become a diehard fan who eagerly waited for him to rob a church. As a young girl, Sara grew among the shadow of criminals and was excited to hear about the underworld. That's why she became a Private Investigator and stayed close to that world but within her legal rights. As a part of solving cases, she read lots of books on crime and mystery and Godless was like one of her favourite characters that had come to life. She often fantasized about him, although she had no clue who he was. The tattoo of a book on the neck was her love towards reading.

In few days, the search for Godless tightened and the security increased. There were many more check posts installed in various parts of Goa to get hold of Godless, but it did nothing than increasing traffic jams. This news had now spread across India and many news channels broadcasted it in their own ways. Some said Godless was a Hindu, some said he was a Muslim, and some said it was a gang and not a single person which gave rise to many protests and riots in different parts of Goa. This diversity of caste resulted into riots and marches in the different groups of the society and to put an end to it, a special cop, Mr. Bhatnagar was called in from Mumbai.

A cop with an exceptional record. Mr. Bhatnagar was in his forties and had linkage to the disappearance of a famous hitman "Jaggu" in the 80s in Mumbai. Godless and Jaggu had similarities, both of them were super smart and expert in wearing disguises. It was in the news that Mr. Bhatnagar was the one who tracked Jaggu from the tattoo of a gun on his left ankle and took him down and this is why he was sent to Goa to track and find another outlaw. People said he was "The Chosen one" and if anyone could end this chaos, it had to be him.

Arrival of Mr Bhatnagar was a huge thing and again the media stepped in and made a massive thing out of it. They broadcasted it live on Television which in turn helped Godless. The media gave away many details about the ways Mr Bhatnagar operated and the Godless noted them all. This didn't bother Mr Bhatnagar. He was cunning and ruthless to both the criminals and the cops, and every single cop wished they weren't made part of his team. This case was being tracked at the highest level and hence on the direct orders of the home minister, Mr. Bhatnagar was given control of all the stations in Goa. It was believed to be the beginning of the nightmare for the criminal and the cops.

On his first day, he called a meeting with the cops Incharge of all the twenty stations where the Godless had hit so far. This meeting was scheduled at the station in Panaji. He asked them to carry every precise detail they had on Godless. He wanted to review everything before laying his trap.

"Alright, let's start, fill me in," said Mr Bhatnagar. All the cops looked at each other but nobody spoke and how could they, they had nothing to show for the past seven months since the reporting of such theft started.

"Okay, let's start one by one" Mr Bhatnagar asked the first cop among the twenty to start. He was from Bicholim, a little place in north Goa and the among the first ones to receive a complaint about a theft in the church in his zone.

The cop stood up and said, "We were the first one that officially registered the complaint about the Godless. Initially we assumed it was someone from the parish and so we spoke to all the families and searched all the corners in Bicholim but found nobody suspicious. This being a small church, we didn't install any cameras. People here are god loving and I confirm its no one from there" Mr Bhatnagar wasn't pleased.

"Bicholim, did u check for any fingerprints?" asked Mr Bhatnagar.

"No sir, we didn't, till the time we could think of it, it was too late" replied the cop.

"Were there any other such complaints?" asked Mr Bhatnagar. "No sir" replied the cop. Dissatisfied with the response Mr Bhatnagar asked the next one.

"Let's move on and as per the list with me, its Bambolim. Get up Bambolim and please share your finding" Mr. Bhatnagar started addressing the cops by the location they represented and not by their name. This was insulting to the cops, but they swallowed these insults and went on.

"We are the ones who confirmed that the Godless was a male and was working alone. We found a pair of shoes which didn't belong to anyone in the entire parish" replied the cop from Bambolim with a smirk on his face assuming he impressed Mr. Bhatnagar.

"You mean to say, a man stole from this church and on his way out left his shoes. Please correct me if I am wrong. Your only conclusion or should I say contribution to this case is the pair of shoes?" asked Mr Bhatnagar.

"Yes sir, its number nine. We also checked nearby bars and restaurants to find out if anyone lost their shoes, but nobody came in front" replied the cop from Bambolim.

"Okay, tell me genius, did u try to find out how many people in your area wore number nine shoes and did u try to find out the shop who sold them?" asked Mr Bhatnagar.

There was silence in the room "no sir" replied the cop from Bambolim.

"Okay, where are those shoes now? can I see them?" asked Mr Bhatnagar but there was no response from the cop. His head was down. he was feeling sorry for something. Mr Bhatnagar wasn't sure and so he asked again, "what's the matter? do you have the shoes or not?"

"Sir the shoes were number nine" replied the cop.

"Yes, you told us, "said Mr. Bhatnagar.

"My son also wears number nine" this response from the cop was merciless.

"You mean to say, your son is the one we are looking for?" asked furious Mr Bhatnagar.

"No, No, No. I am trying to say that my son is wearing those shoes now" replied this cop with a lack of enthusiasm in his voice.

There was silence in the meeting room. Everyone knew this was stupid thing to do and all the eyes were dead set on Mr. Bhatnagar to see how he reacted.

"Sorry sir, we didn't think it would go this far" replied the cop from Bambolim.

"You are sorry? don't be sorry. It's not your fault that you are so stupid. How did you even get this far. Do one thing, get out of my face and don't ever show me that ugly face of yours" yelled Mr Bhatnagar and the cop ran out of the door. This scared all the other cops in the room. They all knew how arrogant he was, but this was too much of pain to go through. It felt like an interrogation. Goa was always a place to settle for a calm life and these cops were never treated this way.

"Reponses from both these cops is bullshit. I can't believe how they couldn't find anything. Stupid, good for nothing cops. Who's next" asked the ferocious Mr Bhatnagar. Nobody stood or even acknowledged. He asked Again and again there was no response. Then from the corner of the room one cop raised his hands. It was shivering but he still raised it. This cop was the youngest one in this group possibly around the age of twenty-five. Mr Bhatnagar expected him to come up with something that can be useful.

"What's your name and where are you from" asked Mr Bhatnagar. This cop stood and still his hand was raised.

"My name is Xavier, and I am Incharge of the Agonda station" replied Xavier and his hands were sill raised. "Godless hasn't robbed the church in Agonda yet but I have a theory about him. If you allow me to speak about it".

"You are lucky I guess that Godless hasn't robbed your church so far, but what theory could you possibly have? Go on…spill it" replied Mr Bhatnagar. While signalling Xavier to put his hands down which Xavier didn't understand and still raised his hands.

"I think there is no Godless. I think this is just an illusion created by some of the local parishes to hoard in more of the insurance money. I traced back to the early days of these robbery and the money collected weren't insured back then. But as the news of initial robbing spread, the number of insurances increased in Goa. What if the churches did this on purpose with an intent to cover their black money and to produce false insurance claims? After all nobody is not that smart to rob so many places and not to leave a single clue. I mean I cannot digest the fact that nobody even has a glimpse of it." Xavier than looked around the room and everyone was stunned. Their expression was weird and one of the cops voiced out, "What the hell are you talking about? Are you trying to say that this is all just a stunt by the priests? How can you blame the messenger of God with such an ungodly act"? Few more cops then started shouting at Xavier, but the Mr Bhatnagar silenced everyone.

"Its too early for me to comment, but I think this could be possible. All the parishes report into same roof and we cannot discard the possibility of this being an inside job. But like I said its too early for me to comment" Mr Bhatnagar was impressed by this theory and decided to get to the root of it but did believe Godless existed.

"Anyone else has anything to add. So far we've been in this room for more than an hour and have nothing that can help me catch this guy".

Nobody responded. Mr Bhatnagar got the gist of it and assumed these cops were useless to him. He then got up from his seat and walked up to the window. While looking out of the window, he asked all of them to vacate the room and looked at the list. He was on his own now and with all his experience, brainstormed into identifying patterns and predicting the stealers next step. This was something he learned at the academy. At first, he thought maybe Godless targeted places alphabetically. Both these locations started with the letter, "B", but then after going through the list he was convinced that wasn't the way Godless operated. Bambolim was on the opposite side of Bicholim, and Mr Bhatnagar couldn't find the relation between them. The flaw in his thinking was that he was overqualified to think like the Godless and on the other hand Godless was simple but a smart ass.

The first day for Mr Bhatnagar ended the way it started, clueless with no plan of attack. On the second day of the arrival of the Supercop, the station in Panaji was surprisingly visited by the priest and bishops from various parishes across Goa. This gathering was not only to vent out their frustration but also to pray for Mr Bhatnagar's success. The priest and the bishop were the most respected people in Goa and hence nobody stopped them from entering the room where Mr. Bhatnagar was busy with his team working this case. The door was pushed open by one of the priests and ten out of fifty entered the room. All the cops in the room stood up and Mr Bhatnagar approached the priests.

"What is this nonsense, who allowed you to come in" asked Mr Bhatnagar furiously and asked them all to get out.

"Son we came in to pray for you and to wish you success. This Godless guy Is a sinner and must be punished. He Is the demon that has contaminated this sacred land of God" replied one of the priests.

"Goa, a sacred land of God, are you joking?" asked Mr Bhatnagar and added, "People here drink alcohol like crazy, everyone knows what happens at the rave parties and not to mention the casinos? what is so sacred about all of it?"

"We didn't build this, it's the people from outside that came in and spoiled the beauty of Goa and this sinner is doing the same. We want him caught if not dead." Saying this "In the name of the father…" started praying that's when Mr Bhatnagar yelled "stop, take this back to your churches, I don't want all this here".

There was silence in the room and all the eyes started Mr Bhatnagar. Then a cop named Fernandes whispered, "sir, let them get it over with, it will take only few minutes. This investigation will get difficult if we go against them".

Then all the priest prayed for the end of the reign of Godless, sprinkled the holy water across the room and then they left.

"Hold on guys" on their way-out Mr Bhatnagar said, "All of you are here, and this is on the news too. Let's hope Godless Is not taking advantage of this situation. Who's watching your churches now?".

This scared all the priest and they scattered back to their churches. This comment started off as a joke but what the Supercop said, happened. In few hours another report of a church being robbed came in. Once this news reached Mr Bhatnagar, he immediately left for the location of crime with his team.

The latest victim was the Church just on the other side where Mr Bhatnagar was stationed. This was either an open challenge to Mr Bhatnagar or foolishness of Godless. The cops took over the entire church in the next forty-five minutes. Every corner was checked but again they found nothing but disappointment. Mr Bhatnagar then checked the camera and wasn't surprised to see a man walking out of the church through the back door. The picture wasn't clear, and this man was in disguise which made it impossible to identify. He asked his team to go out the backdoor and check if anything of use can be picked up. Then walked into the room where the money was stolen from. Me Bhatnagar asked the priest, "How much did he steal?" and the priest replied, "around one lakh".

This didn't convince Mr Bhatnagar. Today was Tuesday and there weren't any sermons or gathering of people which could generate such a huge amount.

He asked "how come you have that much of cash available in the church that too on a Tuesday. Looking at the hall, I doubt more than fifty people could have gathered here" Mr Bhatnagar doubted every word that came out of the priests mouth. "I suppose you have insurance right" asked Mr Bhatnagar and the response was "yes" from the priest. "Did u hear a place called Bank, put your money in the bank, its safe there". Then the cops cleared the place and walked out.

On their way out, one constable asked Mr Bhatnagar, "sir what do you think?" and he replied "This is all bullshit. Maybe Xavier was right. It doesn't make sense. For all I know that this priest is a fraud and was lying to steal the insurance money. Can you imagine this place having that much cash lying around to be stolen? And secondly, nothing is messed up, it's all too clean".

The constable nodded "Humm, you may be right sir, this place is too much of a risk and too small to be noticed".

While they were walking towards the car, Mr Bhatnagar kept on thinking about Xavier's theory of Godless not being a real person. Maybe he was right, maybe it's just a character made up by the priest to hog in more money. After all the priest himself said this money was insured. One thing was clear that he didn't trust anyone around here, especially the priests. Then out of the blue he laid his first trap.

"Hey, come here, I want you to go to the press and tell them to release a statement saying that today Godless stole one lakh from this church and on his way out he killed a man" he asked his constable to release this fake story hoping the Godless would fall in his trap and try to contact him to clear his side of the story.

"Why to mention he killed a man sir, we all know he has never hurt anyone or even damaged anything, then why turn him into a killer? asked the constable.

"Nobody has seen Godless right. He robs during daytime and still nobody sees him. There is no proof if this guy even exists. If he does, he would be too proud of his achievement and wouldn't want him tagged a murderer. If he is real, he will reach out" replied Mr Bhatnagar hoping this guy was real.

This statement was out in couple of hours and was running on all the leading news channels. On his second day, Mr Bhatnagar made his mark. He announced his arrival with a bang. All his colleagues and off the case cops were stunned. They knew his ways of dealing with situations was bizarre, but this was clearly a lie which could backfire if the media got to the root of it.

That evening nothing else happened. At the sunset, people went back to their homes. Godless didn't make any move either. Mr Bhatnagar went back to his cottage arranged by the Goa government near Dona Paula. It was a standalone house with a cook and an old security guard. That night on his way, he took a bottle of whiskey and a novel home with him. It was a book on the story of a thief. He went through it in the night hoping to find something that can help him track Godless.

Just like the previous day, there were people who had come to meet Mr Bhatnagar. This time it wasn't the priests or the local politicians it was 'Savours'. Mr Bhatnagar walked into the station and was shocked. He was upset to see how easily these guys walked up to the station. It was like the cops had no command over them. There were more than twenty bikers in front of the gate. The Saviours wanted their present felt and so they continued running their bikes in circles outside the station. Mr Bhatnagar was in his office and this noise frustrated him. It was unsettling his thoughts. But he ignored them. The bikes blaring from below was loud enough and the smoke emitted from the bikes curled in through the window. It had Mr Bhatnagar's attention now. He walked up to the window and looked outside. He saw nothing but smoke. Then he walked outside where the other cops were trying to control the situation.

"What the hell is happening and who are these hooligans" asked Mr Bhatnagar to his colleague Fernandes.

"They are the Saviours" he replied.

"Good for them, what do they want and why are they here" asked Mr Bhatnagar.

"Sir they want to meet you, it's about the Godless. Their leader wants to talk to you in private".

Mr Bhatnagar looked at Fernandes "Nowadays everyone wants to talk about the Godless. Anyways, who's their leader, call him".

Leader of the Saviour stood across the barricade and Fernandes signalled the leader to approach. "Please take off your helmet," said Fernandes.

The leader took off the helmet. Mr Bhatnagar was surprised to see a girl leading this gang. "What is your name and what to you want to talk about".

"I am Sara. You said Godless killed a man. I want to see the proof and also need details of the person whom he killed" replied Sara.

"Are you crazy? Don't waste my time. This is none of your business. Get lost and take your gang with you" Mr Bhatnagar sounded furious but that didn't scare Sara. She stood there with couple of gang members.

"I am a private investigator and can help. I just need to know if I can trust you" replied Sara.

"Trust me or don't, I don't care. Now get out before I take action" This was too much for Mr Bhatnagar to take and he was losing patience. He also called in few more cops just in case they were needed.

Then Fernandes whispered to Mr Bhatnagar, "Sir coordinate with them. This gang helps us in many cases and has excellent network to track criminals. We might not be able to crack this case without them, but this investigation will surely get difficult if we go against them"

Mr Bhatnagar starred at Fernandes with anger burning in his eyes. "You uttered these exact same words when the priests were here. Are you really a cop?". Fernandes looked down in shame.

"Come, let's talk in my office" said Mr Bhatnagar but Sara denied.

"I have never walked into a Police station and don't plan on entering one anytime soon. "Let's go".

Sara turned around and kick started her bike. Once she saw Mr Bhatnagar on the backseat of her colleague's bike, she drove away. They stopped at the nearby diner. Only Sara and Mr Bhatnagar walked in. They sat at a table in the corner and started their conversation.

"Why did you start the rumour that Godless killed a man. Everyone knows he didn't. He is not a murderer" Sara started the conversation and immediately this made Mr Bhatnagar uncomfortable.

"Looks like you know him very well. Am I missing something?" he asked and added "See lady, I came here not because I am scared of you or your gang, but only out of respect to you. Don't consider this my weakness. I don't have to explain my way of working to you or anyone else. Now if you have anything that can help me catch this guy, please share else I am out of here" Mr Bhatnagar stood up to walk out but Sara stopped him. "Wait, I have some photos to show to you. Don't know if this could help"

This got Mr Bhatnagar excited. At least someone had something on Godless. He sat down and went through them. These were few photos of some tourist who was seen at multiple places and that too alone. Sara and his gang followed him many times but every time he got away and his current whereabouts were not known. These photos weren't clear, but Sara thought the guy in the photo was Spanish or from Australia and maybe he was the Godless.

"Thanks, I will take it to the immigration and get their details. Anything else?" asked Mr Bhatnagar and stood up again to walk out.

"Do the right thing, don't make a killer out of him," said Sara.

"If he is real, he will contact" saying this he turned around but bumped into another guy and spilled the coffee on both of them.

"Sorry bro" said this guy, but Mr Bhatnagar ignored him and walked away.

"Here take this" Sara handed him a tissue to wipe the coffee that was spilled. Then Sara stood up and just as she walked away, this guy complemented her Jacket.

"It's an amazing Jacket and the colour suits you. I mean my favourite colour is also red, but it suits you better. And that's a unique tattoo. You look good. Thanks for helping me with the tissue". Sara smiled and left.

Sara noticed few things about this Guy. He was wearing jeans, white T shirt which had turned brown as the coffee was spilled all over it, a black jacket, a hat, and his long hair curled out of it. The lenses he was wearing had design of a panther's eyes which caught her attention.

On her way back to her gang she received call from Mr Bhatnagar who sounded like he was rushing into something. "Hey this is Bhatnagar, wait there at the diner. I'll be there as early as possible"

"I just left, why what happened?" asked Sara.

"It's Godless, he's there" he yelled.

"How do you know its him. Did he tell you it's him" Sara asked sarcastically?

"I know its him, wait there, I am coming," said Mr Bhatnagar.

Immediately Sara turned around and was sure that this guy on whom the coffee was spilled was Godless. But by the time she reached there Mr Bhatnagar reached too. That guy was nowhere to be seen. They both asked people inside and outside the diner, but he was gone. The camera didn't catch him either.

"How do you know he was here?" asked Sara.

"Who else would it be? he left a note in my pocket".

He handed the note to Sara, and it said. "I am not a murderer. Don't make me one".

"hmm" Sara was surprised but also had a doubt if this note was really from Godless and if he really was here. "What if this guy was just delivering this note. Why to risk getting caught?" Sara left the diner immediately.

Mr Bhatnagar was convinced Godless existed. This made him furious and out of frustration he started throwing chairs around and stopped when he realized the media was taking his photos. All the actions of Mr Bhatnagar's fury were recorded by the media who were sent in by Godless to capture the expressions of a failed and embarrassed cop. In the eyes of others this move back fired but for the super cop this was a success. At least now he knew he had to catch a real person.

Sara was on her way back and thinking about Godless when she felt a sudden shiver in her body. She was already Fantasizing about him and now the Fantasises were turning into love. She was falling into love with Godless. A man she had never seen.

On the other hand, Mr Bhatnagar's little episode of "venting out the frustration" was all over the news with a headline "When cops went Crazy". This was a huge embarrassment for the police and this matter immediately escalated to the home minister who demanded explanation from Mr Bhatnagar. But he convinced the home minster that his plan worked and the Godless did reach out to him. This had never happened so far. With an ultimatum, Mr Bhatnagar was given a last chance to catch Godless.

It was Christmas time now and some say it was the last time when they heard about the stealing. Entire Goa was lit up with decorations and with beautiful cribs outside their houses and the churches. Mr Bhatnagar continues his investigation, and this night was Christmas, he was confident to strike gold.

Saviours had given up the search for Godless and It was only Sara who persuaded to find him. During Christmas time, Sara was alone as most of her friends were with their families. Some even invited her to spend Christmas with them, but she denied. She spent most of her time doing charities like giving away food and clothes to the poor. Sara wasn't a regular visitor at the church but since the rise of Godless, Sara frequently visited churches not only to pray to God but hoping she could meet her crazy fantasy. Now that she was alone, Sara visited many churches on this day of Christmas and helped the staff with the decorations. That's when she noticed the presence of cops in few of the church premises. She approached one of them and asked the reason behind it and only after taking a bribe, they mentioned about laying a trap for The Godless. Someone anonymous had tipped off the cops that Godless was going to hit multiple churches on the night of Christmas, but Sara didn't believe that. Yes, the money collected could be extremely high, but she felt like the Godless won't be active on the night the God was born.

Mr Bhatnagar and his team were still searching for Godless who continued robbing churches and getting away. This was Mr Bhatnagar's last chance. His earlier plan of spreading a rumour that Godless had killed a man, backfired. Mr Bhatnagar also had to issue a public apology for same. This was now personal for him as his reputation of being a Supercop was on the line.

Madness of catching Godless had possessed Mr Bhatnagar and he drowned himself into analysing the reports, going through every statement, every photo and tracking the live street cameras across Goa. He locked himself in his office for days and one fine day, got a tip that Godless will attempt to rob more than one church on Christmas. He was informed that Godless had teamed up with few more and this heist on Christmas could be his last one in Goa. It was four days to Christmas and Mr Bhatnagar had deputed all of the police staff to all the major churches in Goa. These cops were given a task to go through the list of parishioners, to talk to them one on one to understand if they had any clue and to install cameras at the churches with a capacity to hold more than five hundred people. This scared many families and again Mr Bhatnagar's way of working was under scrutiny.

On the night of Christmas, Mr Bhatnagar was busy watching the screens of the sermons from different churches where cameras were installed. He was glued to his seat and talking to the cops on the radios. Not once did he get up from his seat and was continuously communicating with his team. In some time, he got frustrated. There was nothing to report. None of his teams had noticed any unusual behaviour nor nobody reported any suspicious activity the entire night. Finally, the sermons ended, and everyone celebrated the birth of lord Jesus. The skies were lit up with fireworks and there were people celebrating out on the streets. It was like a carnival.

Everyone was happy except Mr Bhatnagar. This was his last chance at redemption, and he failed. The next morning, he arranged a conference call with the heads of the few police stations to see if any church reported a case of getting robbed. But nobody did. Again, Godless was step ahead and again the theory of Mr Bhatnagar proved wrong.

In few months the Robberies in Goa had subsided, and the super cop Mr Bhatnagar was transferred back to Mumbai. Sara was sad with the disappearance of Godless as she never got to meet her fantasy in person but was relieved that things were getting back to normal in Goa and they had gotten rid of the so called 'Super Cop'.

After couple of years, to celebrate her colleague's birthday, Sara took the Saviours to a place which was known for partying and that's where she met someone who completed changed her life.

There were twenty members in the gang, and they all were dressed in traditional black jeans and leather jacket. Like always Sara took over the situation and handled everything. These guys were rebellious but still had the decency and respect for the staff and other's around. The owner of this place observed them for some time and then approached Sara to introduce himself. She was wearing her signature red jacket.

"Hi, I am Austin, owner of this place, do let me know if you need anything".

Sara looked at him and took the helmet off. Austin saw her beauty and just like that fell for her.

"Hey, thanks" she replied and got back to settling her gang.

Sara replied with a sarcastic smile which Austin thought was rude and he felt insulted. He turned around and walked back to the bar from where he continued watching them. Austin had fallen for Sara as soon as their eyes met. It was "love at first sight". Austin was also impressed with the gang. Their attire and their attitude of "we just don't care!". This was something new in Austin's life and he wanted to be a part of it.

Austin was a rich man staying alone in his huge mansion up on the hills. He was a carefree bachelor and a successful hotelier. But it wasn't an easy ride for him. He broke his back to get from rags to rich. He had so much money but no time or family to spend it with. With all the rush in his life he hardly got time to enjoy his life and barely had any friends. Austin desperately needed a break. He had the money, colleagues, accomplices but no friends and that is why he eagerly wanted to be a part of this gang. He was kind of a loner and wasn't social. There were many secrets to Austin's life and one of them was that he didn't know how to ride a bike. To be part of a biker gang it was obvious that one needed to know how to ride a bike. Nobody would carry him on his backseat. Austin excelled at many things in his life, but he failed at cycling and hence feared driving a bike. 'Balancing' was his major concern. Now, if he had to be an active member of this biker gang, he had to overcome his fear and learn to ride a bike. And so, Austin got busy with his planning while the gang continued their drinks and dinner.

Austin was busy sipping whiskey when in some time Sara approached him.

"Hey, sorry for earlier. You were decent to introduce yourself and I responded rudely".

"Don't say sorry. You were busy settling your team and needed a breather" he responded with a smile on his face and added, "would you like to have anything? it's on me" and they both shared a laugh.

"No, that's fine" she replied.

"Please, I insist. Anything that you want. You can have it"

"As tempting as this offer is, I would have to decline. I'm driving you see" she replied but Austin wasn't giving up.

"it's just one drink. What harm could it cause? I'm sure you can take care of yourself". Austin insisted signalling the bartender to make a drink.

"It's not me that I'm worried about. It's the people around me". She smiled said 'goodbye' and turned around to leave.

"At least tell me your name. I have the right to know who refused my offer for a good time." Austin was desperate.

She turned back and said "Sara".

This little conversation ignited a spark in them. They sat seven tables apart but still glanced at each other frequently. It was a magical evening which unfortunately had come to an end. In sometime post finishing their food, the gang left. But that wasn't the end of this story. Although Sara didn't leave any contacts to get in touch with, Austin had a feeling she would come back, and he had to be ready when that happened. So next morning he bought a bike and approached one of the staff member Franklin to help him learn.

Franklin was a kid in his early twenties and was new at the hotel. He was one of the staff who travelled through bike and hence was picked by Austin. An aspiring stand-up comedian, he also performed stand ups on weekends at the hotel, that's when Austin saw him the first time. Austin did a background check on Franklin and learned he was a bachelor which made him a better choice. Austin knew he would definitely have a good time if Franklin agreed to teach him to ride a bike.

Learning bike wasn't a big thing for Austin. With all the money he had he could easily walk into a driving school and get it done, hell he could buy a driving school for that matter, but he didn't want people to know about this embarrassing disadvantage. 'A rich hotelier who can't ride a bike' wasn't something he wanted to be known for.

When Austin approached Franklin, Franklin had no other options but to agree. Denying Boss wasn't a good thing for his young career and Franklin knew that. He immediately agreed to both, teaching to ride a bike and to keeping this secret from others.

Austin owned a property on the hill outside the city and that evening he drove there in his Jaguar while Franklin took the bike. Austin's house had a huge backyard where he planned to overcome his fear. He showed Franklin the place where they could conduct this training. It was behind this huge mansion.

Austin was proud of his house but today it looked like set of a horror movie. Not at all friendly for the first timers to learn a bike. It wasn't lush green but a muddy one with lots of sands, bottles, boxes and what not lying around. Condition of this ground was bad while the chances of getting severely injured was extremely high. Especially if you were going against gravity. Franklin saw Austin from the corner of his eyes and got a feeling that this condition of the field embarrassed him. It was more of a shock than embarrassment. Austin just stood there looking at the mess. His expression said he wasn't aware of what happened there. Austin was forced to reschedule the practice.

"You may go now. I will let you know when we start," said Austin.

"Sure sir, good night" replied franklin turned around and left.

He started the bike but instead of going back to his place he decided to take a little tour of this gigantic place. He drove around the house and peaked in trying to see the inside of the house. What he saw next astonished Franklin.

This yard was a huge one but as it had gotten dark, he couldn't see the inside of it clearly. Then he walked to the other side where he had a clear view of some rooms and realized what he saw some time back was just a tiny little part of this humongous house. Peeking inside the house from behind the bushes and the trees continued and that's when he saw a kid inside. This surprised Franklin. Everyone knew Austin was a bachelor and stayed alone then who was this kid?

Somehow without tripping the alarms Franklin jumped across the fence and looked inside from the window. Franklin was clueless on what was happening here. There sat a kid on the bed, ageing somewhere around ten or eleven, playing with toys and then Austin walked in. In sometime both of them left the room and walked to the kitchen. Austin served food for them both and they had dinner.

Franklin was peaking in now for almost twenty minutes and hadn't seen anyone else around. No parents nor any servants. Franklin thought maybe the servant would join in later when the dinner starts but he was astounded to see Austin taking the food out of the fridge, heating it, and serving it to the kid. They both ate the food and Austin even washed the dishes, cleaned the kitchen platform, and then carried the boy to the room upstairs.

What was this all about? Franklin was blown away. Was this kid adopted or dumped on Austin by some girl for not using protection during coitus? Only Austin had answers to these questions and Franklin was scared to ask.

On the other hand, Austin assumed Franklin had left. He had no idea Franklin was secretly peeking inside his house.

So far for Franklin this was too exciting to leave but hiding there wasn't easy. Franklin was standing in the lawn amongst the bushes and was constantly fighting with the insects and the flies.

Then Austin came back down and walked to the front lawn. Franklin followed from outside. Austin then switched on the lights in the front lawn. This lawn was beautifully decorated. Lights were hanging down from the tree and this place lit up as soon as the lights were switched on. He had a bar outside on the lawn, couple of tables under the tree and strangely an open gymnasium. Austin walked up to the bar, poured himself a drink, played on some soft music and then laid on the couch looking at the sky. This was a different side of Austin. So far except the open ground in the back, everything in this house was neat. In the books of Franklin, this mansion was aces.

Franklin saw Austin laying there and sipping away what had to be one of the costliest whiskeys around. He saw Austin's loneliness hidden behind his dominating persona and felt sad for him. Franklin and all the staff at the hotel knew Austin was party animal and hosted a party almost every week. But seeing this, Franklin was in two minds. Was there two side to Austin's life? or was Austin carrying a split personality?

Austin laid there on the couch for some more time and then got up. Went back inside the house and went to bed. Lights went off.

While Franklin was keen on exploring the secret life of Austin, he had to get back home. He started the bike and was on his way. Franklin didn't realize that the sound of the bike had woken Austin up and he saw him drive away. Austin suspected Franklin was spying and he couldn't allow that.

Next day at the hotel, business was as usual. Austin was there overlooking the operations and then in the afternoon shift came in Franklin. But this turned out to be a terrible afternoon for Franklin. He was fired without giving the reason. This was on the direct orders from the Austin.

This shocked all the staff and there hovered a cloud of uncertainty across the hotel staff. Fear of Austin grew, and the staff was frightened. But this didn't worry Austin at all. He was the way he always was. Evil and cool at the same time.

On the other hand, Franklin didn't get the reason why he was fired, and he could barely overcome this shock. Then after couple of days of mourning he started job hunting. Franklin didn't find any decent job anytime soon after the unfortunate moment of humiliation. This was his first job and it ended without any clue. As bitter as life is, something like this can mentally breakdown any young man of Franklin's age but lucky for him "When god closes one door, he opens another one". That's exactly what happened. Austin had shut down one door for Franklin but had opened another one. This was all part of a plan. Austin's plan to teach Franklin a lesson for peaking inside his house. He showed Franklin who was the "Boss". Then when Austin's anger cooled down, he offered Franklin another job. A job as his 'Personal Assistant'.

After a week of getting fired Franklin got a call from Austin proposing him to come work for him as his assistant. This job was something Franklin had never done earlier in his life and wasn't even qualified for it, but the money offered was much more than what he was earning at the hotel. In the words of Michael Corleone in the movie 'The Godfather', "Austin made Franklin an offer he couldn't refuse."

It's human psychology. Everyone is hungry for money when they first start off their career and here too the greed got on to Franklin and he took the job. Few years earlier similar hunger for money had possessed Austin and look where it got him.

Franklin was the lucky one here. There was obviously something about Franklin that had caught Austin's attention.

Franklin stayed with his family but didn't disclose this news to people around him. There was a reason behind it. He had to share a certain amount of money to his mom out of his salary to run the house and with the remaining he couldn't do much. Now the salary had increased but the money that he gave to mom remained the same there by increasing the 'money in hand'. He wasn't a saint after all.

Today was Franklin's first day of job and he was to report at Austin's house at eight in the morning. It was an hour's drive to Austin's house and so he left home at six thirty. Franklin didn't have any formal dress, so he wore black jeans and tucked in a black shirt. Hopping on his old bike which had an extremely low mileage, he was on his way.

Driving along the empty roads he reached the hills where Austin stayed. There was an old tea stall on the way up where Franklin stopped for a cup of tea and omelette, his favourite breakfast combination. Cheap, easy to cook and healthy at the same time.

Surprising, he didn't see this stall the last time he visited here, maybe he missed it because it was dark. Even today he didn't notice any light bulbs anywhere in this stall. Franklin said to himself, 'why would anybody build a tea stall on this mountain where only one person stayed. Whoever came up with the idea had to be the stupidest man on the face of earth'. Then the man who build it appeared in front of Franklin. This tea stall was old, and it was being run by man way older than this tea stall. He must be in his seventies. At first the old man had hard time understanding what Franklin was asking for.

Franklin asked, "one tea and omelette" and the old man heard tea and chocolate and gave him a candy.

"No sir, not chocolate. I want an omelette. Why would I eat chocolate this early"? said Franklin.

But the old man still couldn't understand. Franklin was sure that as there weren't many customers here the old man had forgotten what an omelette sounded like. But Franklin didn't give up. He tried even harder. Now with hand gestures and signs. His mind was set on eating an omelette and he made sure he got it. Then after some serious efforts, his sign language and body gestures paid off. He got tea and the ever-awaited omelette. Franklin paid him a sum of fifty bucks, sat on his bike and was on his way.

Franklin was punctual and he reached the doorstep of Austin's house before time. But there was something weird about it too. Franklin believed in rituals and to do things on time mattered him the most. Not before, not after but ON TIME. So, he waited outside the door staring at his watch and then rang the bell as soon as it was eight and the maid opened the door.

A week before when Franklin was at this house, he assumed that Austin was staying alone and there were no servants in the house. But today the house was full of them. There were at least fifteen including the security guards. Maybe things changed and Austin might have hired them in this past week just like he hired Franklin. Franklin said to himself 'now this looked like a house of a rich man but where were they that night'?

These servants had one thing in common. They were all young just like Franklin. Everyone was inside the house and gathered around the couch waiting for

Austin to arrive. It looked like Austin had something to address to his servants and so Franklin joined them too. But the kid wasn't to be seen anywhere.

While waiting for the "Boss" to arrive, Franklin asked the guy sitting next to him. "What are you here for? are you new too?" He looked at Franklin like he had questioned his existence in this house and then this guy replied "I'm working here since a year. I am Kalyan, the head chef and in charge of the kitchen and all the servants... since long".

He was the team leader of the house staff and on his response Franklin fumbled.

"I never knew there was a reporting structure of servants too" said Franklin and then looked away.

While Franklin glanced at each and everyone in the room, he couldn't possibly solve the mystery of that night. 'Where were all of them that night and where is the kid now? even the security was nowhere to be seen that night.

Assuming Kalyan would help, Franklin asked, "I was here couple of weeks ago and I didn't see you or anyone else for that matter, even the security wasn't present. How can you leave your boss alone in this huge house on the hills"? Franklin took a high road; he questioned the loyalty of Kalyan who was proud in mentioning his existence in this house.

Now Kalyan had to speak, and he did. "Who are you and why are you here?" he countered back to Franklin. But Franklin didn't respond. "I take my job seriously and staying alone at home was boss's idea.

He gives all of us a paid leave one day every month" replied Kalyan.

Franklin was pleased with his response that gave him answer to the first question "where were the servants?". Now it was time to get the answer for second one, "who is the kid?".

This time Franklin asked him straight, "Since how long is Austin married? looks like he's married young" Kalyan gave the same look and asked, "Bhai tu hain kaun".

Then Franklin introduced himself, "Franklin, PA to Austin"

Kalyan replied, "He is not married, what are you talking about?".

This is not what Franklin wanted to hear. This didn't help. If Austin wasn't married whose kid was that. Franklin had now started doubting on what he had seen that night. 'Maybe it wasn't even a real person, maybe it was a toy. After all Austin was rich and alone and rich and alone people like toys' Austin said to himself. Then there was no more talking while Franklin waited for Austin.

Then the 'Boss' walked down in a black suit looking absolutely stunning, just like James bond. This dashing personality silenced everyone in the room and all eyes were dead straight on him. Few stood up voluntarily and the rest including Franklin were forced to stand up.

On his way down Austin stopped on the last step. Pointed at Franklin and said "Meet Franklin. Your new boss. From now on you need to talk to him even before considering any change. He decides things and his decision is final. Now get back to work".

This announcement dropped like bombs on Hiroshima and Nagasaki. Franklin could see the Cataclysmic change of expression on their faces. They hated him straight away.

But just like the entire staff, Franklin was in shock too. He hadn't signed up for this. Franklin accepted this job assuming he had to handle things related to business, not managing servants at a rich man's house. He wanted to talk to Austin about it and just then Austin walked to Franklin and invited him for breakfast.

Breakfast was held on the front lawn and one servant stood there to greet and to serve Austin. Once the tea was served Austin asked him to leave. It was Austin and Franklin at the table now.

"Are you up for the job" asked Austin.

"No, I'm not, I didn't sign up for this. I thought I would be handling hotel and business stuff. I don't want to handle your working staff at home. I want to handle your working staff at hotel' Franklin responded.

"I hired you as my personal assistant and I'm sure you are educated enough to understand what 'personal' means. Rome wasn't built in a day. Stick around, who knows what's in store for you? If you are indeed a special one, maybe one day, you may end up in my place," said Austin tying to motivate Franklin.

"But why me? you barely know me. I don't have any experience in this and I'm not even qualified. I mean your entire staff is older than me. What do you think I would be able to do here? Tell me why you hired me?" Franklin insisted and was having second thoughts of working here.

"You saw the kid right" replied Austin.

Suddenly the expression on Franklin's face turned from angry to scared.

He nodded 'yes'.

"While sneaking around my house like an intruder" asked Austin.

"yes" replied Franklin.

"People don't do that with me. I do things to these peoples that they couldn't imagine in their worst nightmares" Austin threatened Franklin and Franklin was scared to death. He was practically shivering.

"I'm sorry. It was a terrible mistake, and it won't happen ever again…never… ever". Franklin asked for forgiveness but by the look in Austin's eyes, it didn't seem like he was in the mood to forgive.

"This job is your last chance for redemption. You thought you got this job because you were good, well, you're not. You work for me now and you do as I say and don't even think of getting rid of me. I will find you even if you are hiding in hell and drag your ass out."

Franklin's world came crumbling down. He realized sneaking around Austin's house was a huge mistake and even bigger one was accepting this job.

"It's time to go," said Austin.

Austin was an egoistic person whose money and power had gotten to his head which he used as and when he wanted. Day by day his fear amongst the staff and people around grew. He was even planning to join politics and was super confident that with his contacts, he would definitely win.

What was to be a delightful first day at the new job for Franklin turned out to be a torture. Franklin had no other option but to go on with it and see what happens. Another reason for staying at this job was that the economy was down, and jobs were minimal in the market. Recently he had a bad experience finding a job. Ten interviews and not a single call back. But Franklin didn't know Austin was behind that too. He ensured Franklin wasn't hired at any other Jobs.

Franklin needed a motivation to continue with this job and the money at this job was the only motivation he could think of. But then he saw the other side of it. Standing next to important people could be helpful for Franklin's carrier and this could improve his contacts which a struggling stand-up comedian desperately needed. Secondly how bad could it get? Austin wasn't going to kill him.

"Don't worry I won't go anywhere. I have couple of questions though. I'm sure you could easily hire anyone you wanted for this job then why me? After all you mentioned that I'm not good and secondly who is that kid" asked Franklin.

"Dude! you don't ask questions to me, only I do. Now get started". Austin turned around to go back upstairs but stopped "we leave in forty minutes" and went back to his room.

Franklin acknowledged but he had no clue whatsoever about how and from where to start. Franklin was the boss inside the house, but he didn't feel like it with more than twenty eyes staring right at him and each of them had brutality in them. Like they were going to rip him apart.

"Hi, how are you" Franklin greeted one of the guys to ease the situation, but he didn't acknowledge, nobody did. They didn't care and everyone went back to their work. It was crystal clear message that everyone hated Franklin from the moment they got to know he was their boss. Franklin invaded their space and they wanted him out. But Franklin wasn't going to just sit on it and let that happen. No doubt he had fallen for the money but more than that he was a funny guy who did stand ups and decided to use this capability to win over their hearts. But not today.

While Austin was still in his room getting ready, Franklin wandered around the house looking around. It was the first time he was inside this house and it looked different from the night he peaked in. There were many expensive statues and paintings in the entire room which Franklin was observing closely. Just then one of the servants came with a damp cloth.

"Move, I have to clean this shelf" he said and shoved Franklin away.

Franklin then moved away from the shelf and was looking at the painting in the corner. Just then another servant came with a vacuum cleaner.

"Move, I have to clean the floor" he said and shoved Franklin away. This servant started pushing Franklin backwards and in sometime Franklin was standing outside the house at the doorstep. Then the servant turned around and went back into the kitchen.

Franklin realized this was bullying and he promised himself to turn the leaf around, but not today. Today he had to start off with Austin and so he waited outside and looked around. First time in day light.

Then in sometime Austin arrived. "What do I do sir?" asked Franklin.

"Today you meet people. Come on get in the car".

The car arrived and they both stood there. Franklin was supposed to open the door, but he didn't. Then the driver came out running from the front seat and opened the door for Austin. Once Austin entered the backseat, Franklin followed him. The driver pulled him out. "You come seat with me not with the boss". Then they drove off.

The car stopped at this tea stall on their way down. Nothing was ordered but Austin gave the old man some money. One more strange thing to note for.

Franklin always carried a diary with him. He observed different things and wrote jokes based on them. He wrote down many such abnormal things that he witnessed since morning starting from the tea stall and his struggle for an omelette and was planning on making a series of jokes based on it.

The second stop was at a church down the road next to a beach and about twenty kilometres from his house. Once they reached, Austin got down from the car and while Franklin was about to, "wait in the car," said Austin.

Franklin nodded yes but after some time followed Austin inside the church. Austin went straight to the office while Franklin looked around. Then in sometime Franklin heard the car horn. He had lost track of time and ran back. Austin was already in the car and when Franklin got in, "You do as I say. Don't act over smart. You are not the boss" yelled Austin. Franklin again nodded yes and apologized.

Then they stopped at 'The Elegant' the hotel. It was twelve in the afternoon and most of the staff were busy arranging the lunch buffet. When Franklin walked in, the staff who knew him were surprised. They all knew he was fired but nobody knew he was rehired by the same person who fired him.

While Austin was in the accounts department, Franklin roamed around to meet his friends. Many of his friends were there and few were working the evening shift. They all gathered in the kitchen, and everyone was excited to hear Franklin's story. He told them about how things were since he was fired and how he got this job. "Second guy to the boss" many of his friends only dreamt of it and felt inferior. But then they were all given a reality check when he told them his salary. It was three times more than the senior guy in the room. After a silence for couple of seconds immediately a request for party popped up. Assuring them a party post salary Franklin left with Austin. Austin then took him to the accounts department to complete his joining formalities and then asked him to leave for the day.

Both waited at the valet parking. Austin to get into his car and Franklin to open the door. He was a quick learner and he wanted to show that to Austin. While they waited for the car to arrive, "sir, are you still planning on learning to ride bike" asked Franklin.

"Will let you know. One more thing don't ever come in Jeans again or consider it your last day" replied Austin, got in his car and left.

Franklin thought Austin didn't notice him wearing jeans, but he did and waited till afternoon to let him know this attire was not acceptable. Franklin was surprised. 'Attention to minute details, that's why he was the "Man in charge" Franklin said to himself.

Franklin didn't go home. He went back inside. It was lunch time, and it was time for him to eat what he served few days ago. It was a proud moment for him to be on the other side of food counter. He got himself a healthy lunch, paid for it and then went back home.

Franklin reached home in the afternoon at three and slept for some time. In the evening, first thing he did was buy himself few pairs of trousers and shirts at the nearby shops. When he reached home from shopping, he took out his diary and with the points that he had noted since morning started writing jokes. But then he realized his bike was at Austin's house and catching a bus or a local transport this early was going to be a hell of an ask. Franklin immediately called Austin to let him know he will be late, but Austin didn't answer. There was no way in hell that Franklin wanted to be late on the second day of his job and that too without any information and screw his image. He asked one of his friends to lend him bike for a day. His friend agreed and dropped the bike at Franklins place. Franklin then dropped his friend back home, filled up the tank and relaxed.

Next morning routine was the same. Franklin woke up at the same time and left home at the same time. Halted for a cup of tea at the stall. Today he didn't go for omelette fearing the trouble of going through the explanation like the previous day. Instead, he had tea and some biscuits. Once done he reached at the main gate of the house right on time.

Today Franklin walked in as the Boss and had to show his dominance. First person to greet him was the security guard at the main gate which felt good. He felt proud. Franklin acknowledged him and walked in. Rang the bell to the main door and second person to greet him was the doorman and that was it. None of the other staff welcomed him thereafter. Franklin went in and greeted everyone, asked about how things were and if they needed any help, but the ignorance continued. Franklin cared less about them assuming he had to go out with Austin to handle other office matters. But today was different. On Austin's orders,

Franklin had to stay home. Apparently, this was his time to know the staff and understand his responsibilities around the house. Franklin got scared and immediately a tear rolled down his cheek. All the big talks about being the "Boss" and "Dominating people" went out of the window.

Franklin knew the fact that for an aspiring comedian he lacked social skills of connecting with people and was extremely poor at managing them. He was working hard on improving his communication skills, but it was getting difficult with the involvement of these crazy people in his life.

In sometime Austin arrived and asked Franklin to walk him to the car. Austin told Franklin to give him a clear report of who did what and what changes took place around the house. Franklin acknowledged and when his car arrived, Austin said to Franklin "don't let anyone near the room at the back of the house. It's your responsibility now to guard it with your life". Franklin acknowledged and Austin drove away. 'Guard it with your life' these words gave goosebumps to Franklin. He wandered if Austin meant it or was messing with him.

Once Austin drove away rather than going back inside the house, Franklin went at the back to check out that storeroom Austin was talking about. He also noticed the field where they planned on learning the bike few days ago. It was cleaned and now it looked lushed green. The storeroom was in the corner adjacent to the compound wall and was locked. With nothing to do there, Franklin turned around and walked back towards the house. It was like walking into the den of hungry lions eagerly waiting to rip him into pieces. This was first time Franklin was house-sitting alongwith with the staff. Franklin believed he could turn around things at the house but his assumptions of "things getting easier" went wrong. Today as claimed by Franklin, was the "maddest day" of his life.

The madness started by locking himself out of the house. When Franklin walked out to see off Austin, the staff had the audacity to lock the main door behind him and didn't open despite multiple knocks and bell rings. He tried getting in from the back door but didn't succeed as all the doors were locked from inside. This struggle to get inside the house took him on an adventure of self-discovery where reality started to blend with imagination. With no spare key and no way back in, Franklin sat outside the main door on the porch hoping humanity to step up and open the door for him. But it was too soon to hope.

It was almost two hours now that he was locked outside the house. The sun and the heat were slowly getting on to him. He was sweating from all parts of his body, but he sat there for some more time. Gradually his frustration and the tension elevated to next level, but he didn't react.

In some time, Franklin felt heat in his stomach and decided to go out for lunch. Maybe cool down with few beers hoping the tensions at home to cool down too by the time he got back.

He had two bikes here in the premises belonging to him and it was an easy way down. But when 'It's not your day, it's not your day'. Franklin had left his wallet and the keys to both the bikes inside the house. His formal requests to hand it back to him was brutally denied and so he had to beg to the people inside either to let him in or to hand him the keys and his wallet. This wasn't something that Franklin had signed for and he wasn't here for babysitting some stupid adults who behaved like seven-year-old kids. Then he lost it. Franklin yelled at everyone inside on the top of his voice. He insulted them, threatened them but nothing worked. He went back to sitting at the same spot and then a miracle occurred. A bag with his bike keys and wallet landed in his lap. Franklin sarcastically thanked them and walked towards the bike parking.

The staffs bike parking was on the other side of the main door, so Franklin had to take a right from where he sat. He stood up and walked towards the parking only to see the flat tyre of the bike he came on today. Both the tires were flat. This was done on purpose. Franklin was in no mood to argue so he let this one go by and looked for his other bike he drove in here the previous day. He looked everywhere but couldn't find it in this parking. His bike was not even there in the parking. Again, the staff was responsible for it. This made him really, really mad and he decided to react in a way only these thugs would understand. "Tit for tat" and he decided to do just that. He realized that he was standing in the parking holding these bikes as hostage. He threatened the people inside to hand him bike and belongings else, he would start first by tearing off the seat overs of the bikes, then start puncturing the tires and then breaking the lights.

Initially there was no reaction to this threat but after Franklin repeated it a window opened. Out leaned the head chef Kalyan who asked him to look behind the bunch of trees at the backside of the house and then closed the window. Franklin followed his directions and found his bike in the bushes. First thing he did was to check the tyre and if everything was working. He drove out of the house and on his way down was having second thoughts about coming back. The staff back at the house was super confident that he wouldn't come back.

Franklin stopped at a hotel down the hill and while he waited for the food, he went through the bag. His belongings were safe in the bag, even the money in the wallet wasn't touched. Then he took out his diary and wrote about today's series of unfortunate events. His still had his doubts of going back but as he went on writing he found a funny side to it and his anger changed into 'Experience'. He finished his lunch and went back. It was four now and assuming it would still be locked he sat outside the door. Austin arrived in sometime.

Franklin stood up to welcome him and opened the door which wasn't locked anymore, "you seem wrecked, are you okay" asked Austin and added, "hope everything was fine, and you had a good time knowing the staff".

This was Franklin's time for retaliation. If he wanted, he could have babbled about each and everything that took place today, but he didn't.

"It was all good. I had a fantastic time" replied Franklin while the staff stood there and watched. They didn't understand why he took their side after all they were cruel to him and didn't even allow him to step inside the house for the entire day.

"That's good. You may go now. See you tomorrow" said Austin and he went upstairs.

Franklin went back to the parking and was wandering how to take both the bikes home today. One was punctured off course and it was his friend's bike. Then Kalyan approached. He didn't ask Franklin anything but said to him, "don't worry will get it fixed and drop it to your place till evening".

Franklin was surprised with this concerned behaviour of Kalyan.

"Sure thanks, let me give you my home address" said Franklin and he teared one page out of his dairy and wrote his address, "Don't bother. We know where you live. You will get your bike delivered at home. Remember... WE KNOW... where you live," said Kalyan. Then took the bike keys and went back in.

Was it a threat? On the way back home, Franklin was trying to solve the mystery of how the staff knew where he stayed. Like on the first day, Franklin felt surrounded by mysterious things. Weird things to be more specific. When he got home, he wrote about it in his diary and took a nap. Got up again, wrote few jokes, and went back to bed. End of day two.

Late in the evening the knock on the door woke him up. It was Kalyan who had come in to drop his bike.

"I brought back your bike. You may check," said Kalyan.

"I'm sure it's fine" replied Franklin and just about when Kalyan turned around to leave, "do you wanna come in for a drink" asked Franklin.

"Why not, after all we did to you today, let's celebrate a new beginning" acknowledged Kalyan and as he was stepping in, Franklin stopped him.

"I don't have anything in the house. Please go get it from the shop around the corner" replied Franklin and took the bag off Kalyan's shoulder assuring to look after it.

The expression on Kalyan's face changed. He Murmured, "you invite, and you don't have anything. Stupid!" but he turned around and went to buy a bottle of whiskey.

Kalyan came back in twenty minutes and knocked on the door. Franklin didn't open. Kalyan knocked again but there was no response. Franklin didn't open the door even after few more knocks. Kalyan realized what he did to Franklin today at the mansion, Franklin was doing it to him. Kalyan had the option to leave and get out of there but then he remembered, Franklin had his bag. Kalyan smiled, he got back what he gave to Franklin and confessed, "I understand what you are doing. I get it. Now open the door. let's have this drink. A drink to bury our hatchets and start fresh" Franklin opened the door.

"You are an ass you know that" said Kalyan and stepped into the house.

"I am just returning the Favour as revenge sounds mean" replied Franklin.

Kalyan entered the house and found it to be a typical house of the local residents of Goa. A couch, statue of Mother Mary and Jesus, a rosary hanging from the stand and surprisingly a bar.

"I see, you are stocked," said Kalyan pointing at the mini bar.

"I am in Goa boss" replied Franklin and they shared a laugh.

"You stay with your parents right, aren't they home right now" asked Kalyan.

"They are out of town for couple of weeks" replied Franklin while he set the table for snack and drinks.

When the drinks started, "Family" was at the centre of discussion and they both talked about where they were from and what brought them to Goa. Franklin was born and raised in Goa and Kalyan was from Mumbai. "A lad from Mumbai working in Goa, ideally it's the other way around," said Franklin while Kalyan raised his glass as an acknowledgement.

Then as few more drinks went in, the topic diverted towards "dissatisfied life". Kalyan started off with his tragic story. Apparently, he wanted to become a celebrity chef featuring on various television channels but ended up cooking for Austin. Then before Kalyan drowned himself deeper into the ocean of his 'Disgruntled life' Franklin asked, "why are you all mean to me? have i done anything wrong to deserve it."

Kalyan looked at him "You don't wanna know, leave it. Enjoy your drink" Kalyan denied talking about it but after continual requests from Franklin he spoke. "Don't take it personally. It's what we do to gain trust. It was all just a test, a test to see if you can be trusted and good news bro… you can be trusted."

"That's it! Just to gain trust. What are you in school? This is the stupidest thing I ever heard in my entire life" reacted Franklin.

"It was boss's idea" replied Kalyan.

Then there was silence in the room. Franklin couldn't believe what he just heard.

"Boss's idea! but why?" asked Franklin hoping Kalyan would answer.

"How would I know? He told me to do it and I got the team to do it. No clue why he asked to do it" replied Kalyan keeping himself on the safer side.

They both continued drinking and knowing there is no point in conversing, further the topic changed. After drinking and getting high for couple of hours they called it a night. Kalyan was too drunk to drive or to walk for that matter and so Franklin forced him to stay the night. On the other hand, Franklin was as fresh as the morning sun. Last night's shocking revelation about his boss had alerted all his senses which blocked alcohol from rushing to his head.

Franklin couldn't sleep after this forgettable evening and that wasn't the only thing keeping him up. There was loud noise echoing in the room and that noise was Kalyan's snoring. He snored like a lion's roar, it was like a heavy metal concert in that room. Loud enough to give sleepless nights to Franklin and his neighbours.

It was five in the morning now and Franklin had barely closed his eyes. He wasn't feeling as fresh as he usually is at this time of the morning. Instead, he was hungover and freaked out by the sleepless night. He left the room to get some air and as he stood looking out of the window, Kalyan got up. "Good morning, bro, what a fresh morning. I slept like a baby, what about you."

"I slept like that baby's parents" replied Franklin and gave him a sarcastic laugh.

They had an hour to leave, and it was time to freshen up. There was only one bathroom in this house and they both had to go. Dilemma was who will go first. They both had a strong bowel movement and they both had to go... really had to go.

This was Franklin's house he had the upper hand. But Kalyan was his guest and in India we respect our guests who are 'equivalent to god'. So, Franklin decided... he will go in and the "Guest" will have to wait.

After fifteen minutes Franklin came out of the bathroom relieved and got ready to leave for the job. He came out to the hall but couldn't find Kalyan anywhere in the house. He looked out of the window and there was no sign of Kalyan. Meanwhile, Franklin made tea and an egg fry for both of them and as he was wandering where the hell Kalyan disappeared to, Kalyan walked in.

"Where the hell did you go" asked Franklin.

"You were in the bathroom doing your business, I had to do mine. So, I went outside."

"What do you mean by went outside? This is a gated community" asked Franklin with anger in his eyes.

"You know…went, dumped the garbage, dropped the bomb. But don't worry you won't see. It's buried deep into the ground" saying this Kalyan walked to the table, "shit! forgot to wash my hands" he got up and ran to the bathroom.

"And you call yourself a chef!" murmured Franklin and finished his breakfast.

Then came Kalyan all freshened up wearing Franklins clothes as his were spoiled the night before post spilling everything that they were eating and drinking. He then had breakfast and then they were on their way, double seat on the bike.

On the bike Franklin realized Kalyan too had a weird side and he planned on developing this character for his stand up. Even though the first few days at this new job weren't productive at all, he had received lot of material to improve upon his comedy and this pleased him.

The weirdness of Kalyan kept on evolving and while they were on the bike Franklin felt Kalyan's hands around his waist. Kalyan was handling Franklin's love handles. Instantly the bike stopped. Franklin got down and yelled, "what is the matter with you" Kalyan didn't respond. "I am not gay. Don't fill me up ever again. I will break your hands, I will…" threatened Franklin.

"Okay, okay, I'm sorry. I just got carried away with the morning breeze and the bike ride. Come here give me a hug" replied Kalyan with a huge smile.

Kalyan was gay and his character kept on evolving. Franklin had no problem with him being 'gay' as long as he kept his hands off him.

They continued their bike ride but this time, Franklin kept his shoulder bag between them, blocking any vibe that may pass through.

Like every day for the past few days, Franklin stopped at this tea stall on the way up to the boss's house. Kalyan was a senior in terms of tenure at this job and this was his territory. He had dominance over Franklin when it came to knowing this place in and around and he also knew this old man. So, he took charge. They already had breakfast at Franklins place and Franklin wasn't hungry. He stopped by for a cup of tea. But Kalyan was hungry. He ordered another omelette, couple of sandwiches and tea while the old man gave him the same look as he gave Franklin the other day.

"Oh, sorry I forgot" said Kalyan and then climbed over the table to the other side of the stall and cooked it himself while Franklin stood enjoying the nature. In fifteen minutes, Kalyan brought two cups of tea and scrambled eggs which wasn't what he had ordered in the first place.

"What was this all about" asked Franklin.

"Nothing. He is old and slow. By the time he cooked what I ordered, it would be time for lunch. He has hard time hearing as well. Don't know instead of omelette what else he would have given me" said Kalyan and instantly Franklin replied, "chocolate."

"Huh, what?" asked Kalyan.

"He gives chocolate. You ask for omelette, and he gives a chocolate," said Franklin and added "but you cooked something else from what you ordered".

"I know" replied Kalyan and while Kalyan was enjoying his second breakfast for the morning, Franklin was waiting for him to finish. "Now what?" asked Franklin.

"Now we smoke" said Kalyan and took out a cigarette from his pocket and lit it when he realized he hadn't offered Franklin, "shit I'm sorry, want some?" Franklin nodded 'no'. He didn't talk any further.

Once Kalyan finished his breakfast and smoking, they were on their way.

Kalyan's behaviour changed as soon as they stepped into the house. He wasn't the stupid, idiot annoying man he had been for the last sixteen hours. He had suddenly transformed into a leader who meant business. This impressed Franklin and immediately he sat on the couch took out his diary from the bag and noted mornings incident, every dialogue between Franklin and Kalyan, vaguely off course.

Kalyan rushed back into the kitchen to check on the breakfast as it was the time and Austin hated to wait. On the other hand, while Franklin wrote about the events for the past sixteen hours, he realized Austin was watching him from the floor above. He saw Austin's reflection in his watch and acted like he was deep into thinking about something. His body language and his facial expression changed. Then as Austin walked downstairs, Franklin got up to greet him. "Morning, boss, how are you today."

"Good, c'mon, let's have breakfast" said Austin and approached the table.

"Another breakfast!" Franklin said to himself. This was his third one today. When they reached, there was nothing on the table and just as Austin sat on the chair, out came Kalyan, flying like a superman carrying Austin's breakfast.

"Whoa, right on time" said Kalyan with a huge sigh of relief.

"He does this most of the time" said Austin and laughed.

That moment Franklin realized something. Austin wasn't the way he was acting in front of him. The way he reacted to Kalyan and the way he spoke to the staff showed his softer side. In the house, Austin was a different guy. Maybe the layer of 'Being serious' was just to intimidate the outside world. If this was the case, then Franklin's carrier was in safe hands.

Franklin then took another approach to get close to Austin and to win him over rather than shooting questions about things which he needed clarifications.

For the next few weeks Franklin learned each and everything that he had to at managing Austin's work and managing the staff at home. In fact, he did the job extremely well. His continuous presence and kindness brought him closer to Austin and was now enjoying every minute of his job. For Franklin, "Job Satisfaction" was reality and not a hope.

He even got to go out on a trip with Austin and his rich colleagues. Not to mention the friendship he began to develop with the high-profile people. He had seen all the people Austin met, things that Austin liked to do and not to do for that matter. Franklin was even successful in teaching Austin to ride the bike, but Austin never rode it. He waited for his next rendezvous with Sara.

Franklin was so close to Austin that he even mentioned Sara. Franklin being a good friend offered to help finding her, but Austin denied. Austin believed in destiny and believed that if they were meant to meet again, they will.

Everything was going well but the only thing left Franklin in the dark was the whereabouts of that kid. Franklin had been there for almost couple of months now and never ever saw the kid around. Franklin even tried to collect information through the staff, but nothing worked. Then as time went by Franklin forgot about the kid.

Six months at this job Franklin had lots of memories that he cherished with Austin and with the staff who had become his close friends. His two hundred pages diary was also full of multiple incidents and highlights, but he never really got time to work on his stand ups. Busy routine with no time to work on stand ups, was killing the artist inside him. He realized it multiple times but again got caught into something which diluted the importance and prioritized his job. He had become a workaholic.

Life was wonderful now and Austin's business was booming. Profits were increasing and he planned on taking over few more businesses. But it wasn't a smooth sailing all the way. On his journey to this so called "Greatness" he partnered many crimes but despite all the bad things he did, there was not a single bone of guilt in his body. He lived his life like there was no tomorrow but then something happened.

One day when Austin and Franklin were walking out of the hotel, a guy came out of nowhere and stood right in front of Austin staring at him. The guy was in a bad shape and looked like a beggar. As soon as their eyes met, expression on Austin's face changed. Franklin noticed it. Then they both got into the car and drove back to the house leaving this guy behind. Angrier than before.

Austin was silent all the way which caught Franklin's attention. Franklin even asked Austin about this guy, but Austin didn't reply. A week passed and there was no more sighting of this stranger and things were getting back to normal. But then one fine day this guy was at Austin's doorstep.

He had a proposal that needed an investor and they both discussed about it alone in the room. But then after sometime this guy stormed out in anger. Franklin knew Austin wouldn't tell him anything even if he asked but assumed Kalyan might know who this guy was.

Kalyan had a weak side of blabbering when he was high and keeping that in mind Franklin invited Kalyan to his house for few drinks. That was the evening Kalyan revealed many secrets to Franklin.

After spending more than ten months together Austin and Franklin were close enough where Franklin could ask him questions, he needed answers for, and he did one fine morning over the breakfast.

"You know I saw a kid here one day. Who is he?" asked Franklin.

This time Austin's supremacy didn't work on Franklin, and he had to reveal the long-awaited secret.

"What do you know about my past" asked Austin.

"I know that you came to Goa at a very young age and built this empire out of scratch with your courage and smartness and that you are extremely rich" replied Franklin.

"You got most of the part right. But while building this, I had to offer many sacrifices, crush many people and left many homeless" replied Austin.

"Yes, I'm aware of it" acknowledged Franklin.

"In this rampage I did something to one family that I regretted since it happened but cannot take it back. I took away a kid's parent and his childhood. It was an accident. His parents were killed in a car accident while working for me and he had no one else to go. I took him under my roof. He is staying in a hostel far away at location only known to me and we meet whenever I get time. You know the old man at the tea stall on the way up, that's his grandpa. I asked him to come stay with me, but he refused. He still blames me and curses me whenever I pass by" Austin was in tears after this confession. Franklin had never seen him in tears since he was with Austin. This proved that Austin had a soft side too and that he might be changing for good.

"This is a good thing that you are doing. There is nothing in life than sheltering an orphan and helping him grow. Ask me. I am one of them" replied Franklin.

This shocked Austin, "You're an orphan? But you stay with your mom right."

"Yes but. No idea about my real parents"

Austin didn't intend to dig deep in Franklin's life and so he changed the topic back to the kid.

"You wanna meet him?" asked Austin.

"Yes, I would be happy to," said Franklin.

They decided to visit the hostel that weekend and as the breakfast continued…Franklin shot away the next question.

"Why did you hire me? You never answered that question. I wasn't qualified nor had any experience. Then why me for this Job. You still owe me that explanation". Franklin had asked this to Austin earlier as well but wasn't convinced by Austin's response.

"I guess I can tell it to you now after everything that you know about me. I mean after everything that Kalyan told you, you're still here. You earned it." replied Austin and Franklin was surprised that he knew what Kalyan told him that evening.

Then Austin added, "When I'm at the hotel, I watch every person working for me. Every customer and everything people carry in and out of the hotel. That's when I saw you talking to yourself many times. When I enquired about you, the staff told me that you're an aspiring comedian. That's why I allowed you to perform here for few nights. Things you did, the way you spoke, reminded me of my younger version. Like you I too wanted to be a comedian, spread laughter and happiness wherever I went, but life had different plans for me. Anyway's that's why I hired you and let me tell you, all this time, you did a great job. My decision to hire you was a good one. Happy? now that you know" replied Austin.

This pleased Franklin. He smiled and got up to get things ready for them to leave. Just then "hey, what happened to the stand up? I don't see you performing and didn't even see you practicing. What the hell happened" asked Austin.

"Still working on it" replied Franklin but never told him about the journal and the notes he wrote, "well I too have few jokes which I had written long time back, let me see if I can find it," said Austin.

Franklin acknowledged and walked away into the house to check on things. In some time followed Austin and he went straight to his room to get ready.

That day things were business as usual but with one change. Austin stayed back at the hotel that evening while he asked Franklin to leave. Austin stayed back at the hotel for the first time since Franklin started working for him. Out of nowhere Austin decided to stay till all the guests left. He planned on drowning himself into the ocean of alcohol may be because of the deep discussion he had with Franklin. It was an emotional moment, and he felt a burden was lifted off his chest. Staying alone at the bar wasn't a sound decision, but it proved lucky for him. He met 'The Saviours'. Yes, he met 'Sara' whom, he had almost forgotten.

As soon as their eyes met, Austin walked up to her, "Hey, how are you. Haven't seen you in a long time". There was a huge smile on Austin's face but then it went off when she replied, "Sorry do I know you?".

"Remember we met here at this same place few months back. I'm Austin. I own this place. I offered you a drink and you denied it. You even told me your name "Sara" right.

"Nope no idea. Don't recollect ever speaking to you."

"Okay then, sorry for wasting your time. Enjoy your evening" said Austin and walked away back to his table.

While Sara went back to her gang. Austin glanced at her every now and then and she seemed to be having a good time with her friends.

Austin was busy sipping away his drink when one of the staff approached him.

"Sir, do you want me to refill?"

"Another bottle of whatever this is" replied Austin.

"Sir, may I ask you something" asked the waiter. Normally Austin wouldn't respond, but this time he did "what".

"I noticed that you are looking at this girl for some time now. For the past few weeks, she comes in every Tuesday at eight with her friends and…"

"And what" asked Austin.

"She asked about you" replied the waiter and he left the table.

"What", said Austin and looked up to talk to the waiter but he was gone. Austin called him back to his table. "Sit down, talk to me". The waiter was uncomfortable to sit at the same table with Austin, but he sat anyway. "You said something about that girl asking about me" asked Austin with eagerness in his eyes.

"Sir she comes in every Tuesday with her friends looks around and asks about you" the waiter replied.

"What do you mean ask about me, she just told me she don't remember me. What did she ask exactly"? Austin was curious to know.

"She asked where's your handsome boss?" he replied and added, "maybe it was sarcastic, but she approached me couple of times"

Austin asked the waiter to reconfirm if Sara was that girl "Yes sir, that's her. This is exactly what she said. In fact, she asked me last week. Maybe she was drunk sir, else who would say such things" replied the waiter. Austin acknowledged and signalled him to leave.

Now the smoke cleared. It was a sure thing that Sara was lying about not recognizing Austin and she was playing hard to get. So, he decided to start a game of his own.

For rest of the evening Austin ignored her completely and stayed till the time Sara and her gang left which was at one in the morning. Austin never stayed this late at the hotel and because he was there most of his staff had to wait too. Then when Austin realized it was one, he got up and looked around. Sara and her friends had left already, and he too walked out. Just then things went wrong for Austin.

Tonight, Austin was too drunk to drive or even to walk for that matter. Even his driver was sent home early. Austin had sent him home late into the evening. Austin was all alone and drunk. Still, he got behind the wheels and drove out of the hotel. He could have easily stayed back at the hotel, but he insisted his staff on driving back home.

As he got into his Jaguar and drove away, couple of comrades followed him. They were shadowing Austin for a long time, and this was their best chance to hurt him. As strong and influential Austin was, tonight he was alone and helpless. All the power and money he had couldn't help him.

Austin had no clue that he was about to fall prey to a surprise attack. It was thirty past one now and the roads in Goa were empty. There was nobody to be seen for miles. Austin was all alone on the dark empty roads and that's when these guys speeded up and stopped right in front of Austin's car. At first Austin couldn't see clearly and couldn't recognize them. He thought it was the cops and so he had rolled down the window to talk. When one of them approached the window, Austin came back to his senses and asked, "what is all this, why did you stop me"?

"Get down," said that guy.

Austin denied and rolled the window back up. This annoyed him. He broke the glass with the steel rod that he had in his hand and intended to attack Austin with it. Once the window glass shattered, he accessed the inside of the door, unlocked it, pulled Austin out of the car, and slammed his Austin's head on the bonnet of the car.

There were five of them and Austin was alone. Austin was down and could barely pick himself up. He was down but not out. Suddenly Austin got up and fought back. Even these guys were surprised to see him fight back in such a poor condition. It was five against the one and the 'one' was kicking all five of them. Punches after punches, kicks after kicks, Austin countered every action and paid back with more. His Karate and Taekwondo classes instantly helped him counterattack. During the fight he got his hands on the steel rod and cracked open one's skull which scared the others and they backed up. That's when Austin jumped back into his car and escaped. Austin was tough and he showed that tonight. On the other hand, leaving Austin injured was like a lion who tasted blood.

This wasn't the first time someone had attacked Austin. But like evertyime he managed to escape with just minor injuries. Therefore, he never stayed out late and that too all by himself. It was too dangerous.

Tonight, although there weren't major injuries, he was badly hit on his face which impacted his vision. He couldn't see clearly in the dark and as one of the headlights of the car was broken his vision became shady. Driving steadily in this situation was commendable but then the worse happened. Austin lost control of the car and crashed into a parking full of bikes. His head hit the steering wheel pretty hard and was knocked unconscious. Luckily for him this parking lot was near a 24/7 coffee outlet and there were people who carried him to the nearest hospital. He was bleeding severely but could sense people carrying him.

Next morning at the hospital, Austin opened his eyes. Kalyan and Franklin were beside him at the hospital. Austin asked them how they knew. Franklin said, "someone called our hotel and then the hotel called me".

"Someone, who"? asked Austin.

"That someone" Franklin pointed towards right corner of the room with a smile on his face. Standing there was Sara. Austin's destiny had brought Sara back in his life.

"Sara! hey how did all of this happen and where did you find me" asked Austin.

"Last night after we left your hotel, we went to this coffee shop where you crashed. It was our bikes you crashed into. You damaged couple of them and will have to pay. You owe us two bikes" saying this Sara laughed and so did Austin.

Sara coming back into Austin's life was the beginning of the love story Austin was destined to. But Austin didn't forget the attack on him. He knew he had to put an end to whoever did this before he caused any more damage. Nobody sensed that Austin was attacked. They all thought that Austin was drunk, and the car window was damaged in the accident. He made sure nobody knew what happened that night. Nobody except Kalyan.

On one side, Austin was stepping into a relationship with Sara and on the other hand he couldn't find his attacker. Austin knew it was that guy who visited him at the hotel and then at his home. He was a sneaky guy and getting him out from the hiding was an arduous task. Like Austin he too had connections who helped him hide.

Sara was a regular visitor to the hospital till the time Austin was discharged and they became good friends. She also helped him get home and stayed with him for few hours daily just to give him company. This is when they clicked. Austin told Sara about the time they first met and how bravely he learned to ride the bike just to be a part of her gang. Their chit chat opened lots of secrets and suddenly they were inseparable. Although there was no formal proposal from either of the two, but everyone around them knew they were meant to be with each other.

While Austin was living through the loving company of Sara, Franklin ran the show. He took care of the business.

Sara was a kind-hearted person. Everybody liked her especially Franklin because they both were orphans and shared a mutual respect.

Things changed a lot with Sara and Austin coming closer. For instance, one of the major changes was on the request of Sara, Austin brought home the kid from hostel to stay with him and introduced him to everyone. Sara came to know about the kid's existence when she overheard Austin and Franklin talking in private. Initially she thought it was Franklins kid that they were talking about but then Austin told her.

"There is a Kid, a ten-year-old boy who stayed with me, but I have sent him away at a hostel to an undisclosed location" said Austin and Sara got furious, now she thought it was Austin's kid.

"You have a kid, when were you gonna tell me that, are you married? are you even say what you are? am I just a joke to you" Sara went on like a women possessed and it scared Austin.

"Relax, it's not my kid, I just take care of him. His parents worked for me and died in a car accident. I am not married, phew! why would I keep that from you" replied Austin.

Sara calmed and felt good about this act of kindness. At first because of safety concern, Austin denied but then she convinced him to bring the kid home, to give him a life he deserved.

This kid was named Chris. Chris was seven and as his parents were taken away at an early age, he wasn't the way a seven-year-old kid was supposed to be. He was very quiet and often distracted. Chris was still shaken from the death of his parents and sending him away to a hostel didn't do him any good. He missed his friends and making new friends was something he had no intention of. This homecoming of Chris was possible only because of Sara. She even convinced Chris's grandfather to come stay with them. She was shocked off course, but she didn't care about this white lie. With changes around, Austin changed too. He saw life differently and was involved into many social activities, living a clean life.

Eight months in this so called "Relationship", Sara had become Austin's life. They both helped each other become a better person and their happiness and understanding of each other was admired by everyone around them. Chris was taken care of, and he was closer to Austin and Sara than he was few months ago. Chris had accepted this way of life and was living his long-lost childhood. He was studying in one of the best schools and had many friends. Every month took a vacation with Austin and Sara. They were virtually a "Family".

Sara and Austin had many things in common and one of the things that they both loved was watching movies. Both were crazy movie fans and tonight they planned to watch the movie "Serendipity" and why not they both came close was because of Serendipity. Once the movie was finished, Sara opened up to Austin about something from her past that bothered her, and she wanted to share it with Austin.

"I have to tell you something," said Sara.

"Sure, what is it?" asked Austin.

"That night at the restaurant I was joking when I said I didn't know you. Actually, since the first time we met, I couldn't stop remembering you and I still wander, if I hadn't acted like a jerk, that night would have ended differently, and you wouldn't have to escape death." said Sara.

"Don't worry about it, things have turned good for us. It's not your fault" replied Austin and added, "is this what you wanted to talk about".

"There is one more thing which I want to inform you, it's something that I want you to know before we go ahead in our life. I had a crush I never told you about. That is also the reason why I am not a private investigator anymore," said Sara.

Austin felt bad as he thought he was the only one in Sara life. So, he asked, "when was it and who is that guy? Do I know him. Did I meet him?

"I will tell you but promise me you will not make fun of me" replied Sara and Austin nodded Yes.

"It was few years ago. There was a thief in Goa who stole from the churches and people called him Godless. I was so into him that I wasn't faithful to my profession. I hoped he robbed, and I admired that about it. I was in love with him but one day he was gone. I tried to find him, but I couldn't and that's when I decided it wasn't worth being a private investigator, I think you should know about that"

"Why were you in love with a thief? Isn't it a weird? I had seen such childish crushes in the movies but never heard about it in real life." asked Austin.

"I don't know, it just happened. May be when I began my quest as a private investigator, I stepped into a world of people like Godless and unknowing fell for the one" replied Sara.

Sara sensed a certain amount of uneasiness in the room as soon as she revealed this to Austin and so she asked. "I hope you are okay with it. Is something wrong? I feel you are disturbed by this".

"No, I am not disturbed. I too have something I want to share. Now that we are telling secrets, I have one too and its huge but remember I love you from the bottom of my heart and you will be the only one to know it. I am telling you this because that's how much you mean to me, and I trust you with my life" said Austin and this time Sara looked concerned.

"Don't worry, you can tell me anything" replied Sara.

"You mentioned you had a crush on this Godless guy right" asked Austin and Sara nodded 'yes'.

"I am Godless" replied Austin.

There was silence in the room for few seconds and Sara thought this was a joke. She started laughing. "Yeah, right you are "The Godless". Austin didn't react and kept looking straight into her eyes. Then Sara realized this wasn't a joke, "Oh you are serious" she asked, and Austin nodded "yes".

Again, there was silence in the room. Sara was absolutely stunned and suddenly started shivering. She wanted a glass of water, but her breathlessness made it difficult to cross a distance of four feet, she was having hard time breathing.

"Here take this, breathe into it" Austin gave her a paper bag and asked, "Are you okay".

"What the hell Austin. What are you talking about? Why would you do something like that and why would you hide it from me".

"I know this is too much to take in and I was waiting for the right moment to share it with you. I am sorry to lay it on you like this and I am sorry if this hurts you" apologized Austin and he meant every word of it.

"I bet you already knew who I was and planned all these lies. You made me look like a fool." Sara was furious. "So, this is all built with the stolen money"

Asked Sara and Austin nodded yes but then added. "I had to steal because of the situation that I was in. I am not that person anymore. I have changed, you changed me"

"Do you seriously believe this is something I might be able to forget. You dragged my clean life into this mess. What about the cops? You think nobody would ever know that you stole from their churches, you stole from their God. How long can you run"?

Sara was really going at Austin, and he found it difficult to settle her down. This in fact was a huge thing and Sara's reaction is how a normal person would react. Austin was hoping to end this and was eager to find out what would be her next move.

"Look at me, I am still here. I am not running from anybody and about getting caught, well so far nobody, not even the cops or any private investigator came close. Secondly, I have ensured nothing traces me back to those crimes. Today, I am a clean man with nothing to hide. I never planted any of my moves. Nothing was planned. Falling in love with you was not planned. It just happened. You happened to be there for me. That night of the accident I didn't crash the bikes because I was drunk. It was our destiny. I was attacked by my enemies and was running away from the people who attacked me. I have never loved anyone else in my life. You are and will always be the one. Don't stop it now, let the time take its course, let's see what the world has in store for us". Replied Austin holding Sara in his arms.

Sara had tears in her eyes but now the both of them had vented out, the truth was settling down. Sara was scared and happy at the same time. She was happy because her fantasy had come true. The only person ever she fell in love with was holding her in his arms.

"When did you know it was me and did, we ever cross paths during the reign of The Godless" asked Sara.

"Yes, we met once at a coffee shop. When I was tailing that cop Mr Bhatnagar. You offered me a tissue to wipe off the coffee that was spilled all over me. Remember" replied Austin.

"Yes, I remember. Oh, it was you. The weirdly dressed guy. You wore a hat and some strange lenses. How could I ever forget that look"? Austin nodded "Yes. I had forgotten about you but that day when you walked into the hotel, I saw your jacket and the tattoo on you neck and it all came back. Tell me one thing. Back then at the coffee shop, if you had known that I was the Godless, what would have been your response?" asked Austin.

"I don't know, I mean the situation was different. This corrupt cop had framed you for murder and I was against it. I might have let you go I guess" replied Sara and added, "did you hurt anyone. I mean any priest or the helpers in the church".

"No, I never hurt anyone in the church. Anyways that money was insured" replied Austin and as soon as he thought the "Discussion" about the past was done, Sara asked, "Is there anything else that you are hiding from me? Now is the time to spill it all out. If I ever found out you lied to me, we will be done. That will be end of the road for us".

"Yes, there is" replied Austin.

"Okay, tell me everything, everything from the start, tell me how you got into this, don't leave out anything" Sara replied knowing this was going to be a long night.

"Aright, I will tell you everything, just don't fall sleep" joked Austin and "I won't, I promise" replied Sara.

"My real name is Johnny, born and brought up in Mumbai. I belonged to a working-class Christian family based out of the suburbs in Mumbai. My dad passed away when I was four and I was raised by my working mother and elder brother, Franklin, also known as 'Franky'. I was too young to remember dad, or the time spent with him. For me, dad was just a man in the photo, so I looked up to Franky who helped me improve on my setbacks that he observed in me as a kid. I wasn't into running as I used to get tired quickly for a kid, but Franky encouraged me to run while he rode the bicycle. This was our daily routine in the morning. "Be faster, let go of yourself. Always be the best among the people around you. That will give you an upper hand everywhere you go" this was Franklin's mantra to life, and he trained me to follow the same. Franklin encouraged me to take up sports like swimming, karate and at the same time helped me study. Franklin became my dad and was the world to me. We shared memories of childhood and our

grownups dreams. But it all changed when I stepped into twenties. Our mother passed away with an illness and this is when our life fell apart. I was very close to my mother and had a special bonding with her. Her death shook my entire life. I was barely able to control myself and my life tumbled from excellence to mediocrity.

I became friends with the "Bad Boys" and got into smoking and drinking. My circle of friends changed, and my academic friends alongwith my girlfriend left me as they thought I was pulling them back. Till the time Franky was a bachelor, he cared for me but even that love and affection diluted when he got married. His priorities changed, and I became a burden to him. I was addicted with smoking and drinking and as I wasn't earning, had to beg for money, sometimes to Franky and sometimes to my friends. Soon every door was slammed on my face. My so called "Friends", the ones who got me into bad habits walked away and I was left alone. This hate and betrayal, from my brother and friends boiled inside me like a volcano which erupted one day, and I decided to end it. I even thought of committing suicide but couldn't do it, instead I decided to go away and start a new life, away from my past one. This brought me to Goa and then… the adventure began.

I was twenty-three when I came to Goa. I had no money and so worked at a beachside restaurant as a cleaner. I stayed with few young, debauched boys who just like me had gaping hole in their lives. To stay away from any suspicion, I concocted a story of being an orphan. To them I was a lummox. These guys were pros and probably worse than the guy's I was friends with back in Mumbai. Till this day my bad habits were limited to over drinking and excessive smoking, but I never took drugs. Here I tasted that too. Slowly these roommate's proclivity to drink and take drugs had become part of my daily life. I didn't like drugs and whenever I was forced to consume, my body rejected it and I vomited. This went on for few days and eventually it made me extremely uncomfortable. My roommates forced me to take drugs and when I refused to, there broke out a fight amongst us and it happened many times. I was fed up but as this hotel was my source on income I continued to stay there with limited options. One morning, wearied by the daily squabbles I said to myself 'what the hell, I have left my family and life behind, this job is just another obstacle' and then without informing anyone, I left. I quit the job and moved out, once again…hoping for a better life.

Those thirty days with them alerted my senses and I realized working as a cleaner wasn't something I was born to do. Suddenly, I felt a sort of reverence developing for life and this time I wasn't ready to settle. I was an educated lad and wouldn't settle working as a waiter or a cleaner, I deserved a better job and a better life. I was destined to be a living prodigy.

I had some money left from my last salary and took a bus to Panaji city. A place where I intended to transform, to elevate my life. My mind had opened up, and I started thinking clearly on what I wanted and how I was going to get it. The thirty days' that I spent at the previous place was a wakeup call. My life meant something to me.

Once reached, I busted out afresh from the bus. I was back to my senses but still didn't want any part of my previous life. I wanted to stay here in this beautiful Goa and like a normal man, I was now set out on a quest to find a "Decent Job".

Call centre job boomed in India in the nineties. They paid healthy, so most of the youth opted for it and this attracted me too. These call centres were majorly set up in the metro cities of India and Goa wasn't one of them. However, everyone knew, people in Goa had a good command over English language and luckily for them, one UK based company had set up a tiny little branch in Goa and were hiring. I was good with spoken English and had excellent communication skills. I learned about this vacancy while sipping tea at a tea stall and immediately planned to "walk in" for a "'walk in" interview.

I was confident of cracking the interview rounds, but I had bigger problems to deal with. All my legal documents and certificates were back home with Franky in Mumbai. Even if somehow, I prepared a resume, cracked the interviews, and was selected, I wouldn't be able to produce any legal documents when the company asks for it. That was the first time since I came to Goa, I realized that running away wasn't as bad as compared to running away without my personal identification documents. This was another roadblock and like someone said, 'The road to success… is always under construction', today I realized its true. I was sad and just sat there starring at the mirror in the shop in the front with utter bafflement.

I hadn't contacted Franky since I left Mumbai and wasn't willing to speak to him anytime soon. But I had to get my documents and a visit back at home in Mumbai seemed the only option. But before that, just to get a feel of it I walked to that call centre and sat on the bench at the opposite side of the road. With nothing else to do, I emptied my pockets. There were some candies, something wrapped in a plastic and some money. I put everything back in my pocket except the money and started counting them. I counted the money and as per the availability of finance, planned my next steps. I had exactly thirteen hundred bucks with me which was sufficient for a round trip to Mumbai. But that was all the money I had. I had to spend it wisely considering I had no job and even if I got any now, I would still have to wait till I had salary in my hands. The hotel where I worked, paid daily wages to their employees which surely wasn't in the policy of a call centre. Hence budget planning was extremely crucial.

On the other hand, even if I got my documents and applied for this job, walking in for an interview here was a challenge majorly because of my appearance. My appearance changed with my way of living. I looked like a homeless person and there was no way I was going to get pass the security. In my wardrobe, many of my clothes were torn and the ones which weren't torn, had lost its original colour. Forget the shoes, I was wearing a pair of stolen slippers and not to mention the awful smell my body and my mouth emitted for resisting a bath and brushing for days. I planned on buying some decent clothes and change my appearance to a level where I would be allowed to appear for interviews but there was another problem. What if I failed the interviews? That would be waste of money, and I had very little of it.

My mind wasn't in the right place since childhood. I was different and always stayed in my brother's shadow. Franky made decisions for me for most of my life till. I considered myself smart but immature and because of my inability to think straight, I was in this position. But this wasn't as big an issue as I thought it was. I had a simple solution to all my recent problems. I could patch things up with my brother and still stay in Goa. I could also ask Franky for a loan till I got back on my feet but no... I had to do it the hard way. I decided to go back to Mumbai not to patch up things with Franky but to steal the documents. I intended to steal the documents from my brother's place but to reach his house I needed more money. As I wasn't getting any job anytime soon, my only options for quick money were either to beg or to rob. I was too proud to beg so I planned on robbing. Now I had to rob money to rob documents. I knew it was as dumb and stupid as it sounded, but the man's gotta do what the man's gotta do.

I wasn't a con man and didn't possess the ability to rob people on the streets nor did I have the resources, tools, or knowledge to rob any store or a bank for that matter. But my evil mind knew one place where I could possibly steal few hundred bucks and still getaway. That place was Church.

Growing up in Mumbai, I was a regular visitor to the church and was also part of their groups. I had seen a Church up close and knew stealing few bucks would go unnoticed, nobody would complain. I cursed God for every bad thing that had happened to me in the recent times and my belief in God had died with my mother. So, this was more of a vengeance than just a 'Job'. My indescribable hatred of God motivated me and so with a cup of tea and a slice of cupcake in my hand, analysis of the situation began.

I walked for more than an hour and took a tour of the location. There were five churches within a radius of fifteen kilometres. Stealing five hundred from each of them earned me twenty - five hundred. Imagine this was just fifteen kilometres. There were many more churches across Goa. Stealing five hundred from twenty gave me ten thousand rupees which was sufficient for the Mumbai visit and to spend the rest of the month. Hundred was minimum, but I could go for a higher amount as well. Higher the amount would decrease the number of attempts and the risk of getting caught lowered. Stealing few hundred bucks wouldn't hurt the church.

"Empty mind is a devil's workshop" right, this is exactly what was happening with me. Now I had the 'Why' and the 'Where' and the 'When' was something to work upon.

Suddenly I stopped at a nearby church and walked inside. It wasn't planned but a coincidence. I peeked into the wide wooden donation boxes, but they were empty. May be the boxes were recently emptied and the money was deposited in a bank. I knew there won't be any money lying around in the church, but I could easily get my hands on it during 'offertory'. offertory is one of the activities during the sermon where people donate money. *During offertory, people drop money into small baskets that is rotated around the church. This was it; this was the church where I decided to attempt my first day light robbery.*

It was three in the afternoon now and there was a sermon scheduled in couple of hours. I had enough time to look around and plan the perfect exit.

Entering the church during the sermon with my current appearance was going to be delinquent and so with the thirteen hundred rupees I had, I decided to buy a proper attire. On the other hand, I had to be sure I wasn't over dressed and didn't invite attraction. My spending was limited and was toggling between my desire to buy new clothes and the fear of running out of cash. So, instead of walking into a shop, I walked over to the other side to a seller on the street. There were few of them and they were mostly into sports jerseys or some fancy T shirts with designs saying "I Love Goa" or you know similar type of extravagant messages. I couldn't possibly wear them at church, I would stand out and so continued browsing around when I saw a sky-blue jean lying around. I instantly liked it and tried it on, it was a perfect fit. I had set my mind on purchasing these jeans but was concerned about the cost. So, I asked the seller for its price and the seller replied, "one thousand, sir". I had thirteen hundred with me and if I bought jeans worth thousand bucks, there will be nothing left for buying a shirt, shoes, and socks. There was no way in hell, I was spending thousand bucks on it and that's when my negotiation skills came into action.

My bargaining power took over and I offered hundred bucks to the seller. Seller counter offered nine hundred. I replied with one fifty and this time the seller ignored me completely. I realized this seller was a tough nut to crack and, so I gave my final offer of two hundred bucks, "take it or leave it" and guess what, the seller 'left it'. The seller ignored this offer too and to add salt to injury, he insulted me "get lost don't waste my time" he shouted at me. This was the highest level of embarrassment I had recently experienced, and I understood this is what was in store for me now that I had chosen this life. I could have easily gone back to my brother and started a new life. I wouldn't have to do or even think about doing any of these God forbidden things, but my friend "Ego" had brainwashed me. This insult was personal, but I swallowed this insult and took a deep breath. As I was about to turn around and walk away, I again emptied my pockets to count the money. A candy and the tiny little plastic bag fell off.

I offered candy to the seller which he took without any hesitation, unwrapped, and ate it. Then I digged into that tiny plastic bag and opened it. There was some powder inside it. I spread it over my palm to check what it was. It was white in colour and as I was about to smell it, the seller asked, "do you have more of that".

I was surprised, "Sorry what" I asked him. The seller had no problem in identifying the white powder. At first, I had no clue what it was but then I remembered. I was wearing pants of my drug addict roommate and had seen this white powder before but wasn't sure what it was called. This was one drug which my roommates never forced me to take. May be because it was expensive.

"Do you want it"? I asked the seller and the seller nodded 'Yes'. Immediately the situation changed. I commanded it now. I proposed to trade it for the jeans and even offered to top it up later. It wasn't much but the seller agreed. I got these jeans pant for free but was scared as selling drugs was a criminal offense. I sprinted away from the shop and stopped after ten minutes to another street seller. There without much of bargaining, bought a plain white shirt and a pair of shoes. I bought clothes and shoes worth nine hundred rupees and had four hundred left.

This boosted my confidence to go through this heist. It was critical to gel with the crowd and looking rich would make it possible. Lavish dressing is something the Christians are famous for and now I looked one of them. With only four hundred bucks in my pockets, I had to be successful with this heist, else starving or begging was going to be my new way of life.

I was all dressed up and back to the church where I had to think of a way to get my hands on the money collection bag or the basket. I had two options, either to volunteer for the offertory or to steal the money from the room post the sermon was over. The first option to volunteer seemed a little easy and less suspicious. But to volunteer I had to inform the priest prior to the start of the sermon and the priest must allow it. Generally, only the ones close to the parish or people known to the priest handle the collection boxes. As this was going to be a huge ask and might raise eyebrows, idea to volunteer was dropped. I left it to chance. The offertory comes in around forty minutes once the sermon starts which I knew and so I waited.

It was time now and people started coming in. The church was gradually getting crowded, and I had to find the right place to execute this "day light robbery". I stood on the steps on the church's entrance. There were people standing on the level below as well. This indeed was a big church and could easily fit in about five hundred people. At the offertory, almost everyone pays their contribution, so the amount that is collected at one sermon is huge. Likewise, there were many sermons in a week. I got greedy post calculating the approximate amount of money that this church could generate and the money I could steal.

Then, "In the name of the father, and of the son and of the holy spirit" the sermon started.

I was attending this sermon not with respect or love for God but out of a wicked and a dirty thought of robbing his house. Then as the time to offertory neared the fear and the repercussion of getting caught hovered around which made me uncomfortable. I was scared and was sweating like a pig. Every minute in the church was like a ticking time bomb. People standing next to me glanced at me several times that's when I realized this is exactly what I didn't want... to be noticed!

To stay out of the ogling zone, I stepped away and slided to another corner of the church. Now was the time for 'The Offertory'. One doddering old man carrying the collection bag with a long handle approached the people and people dropped money in it. That's when I decided to make a move. As soon as the old man approached me, I offered him an empty chair asking him to sit while I carried on with the collection. The poor old man was already tired with the long sermon and accepted my offer. Meanwhile, I approached the people on the other side and then the people near the gate. Then just when nobody was watching...I walked out of the church. Nobody saw me. I vanished like a fart in the wind.

I walked away as fast as I could, without looking back. This was the initial idea which I had dropped but it's the one that succeeded. After marching for twenty minutes straight I took shelter at an indoor parking lot. Once convinced nobody was following, I opened the offertory bag and counted the money. It had nineteen hundred rupees, fourteen hundred more than what I had set out to steal. I expected to earn minimum five hundred bucks from this first heist but was amazed to end up with nineteen hundred. Nineteen hundred rupees plus the four hundred I had with me before the heist. It was sufficient to take care of my current needs and requirements.

Befuddled with what I had done, I just sat there at the parking lot for some time. I wasn't feeling guilty but felt satisfied from this act of ungodliness. This only augmented my greed to steal more, and my hunger grew. This was easy money for me and so I planned on doing it again. This time at a new place, new time and at a new church.

I took this cursed stolen money and first thing I did was rent a room for a week. I now had twenty-three hundred bucks with me and was charged four hundred for a week to rent this place. The adrenaline had taken over and I had completely forgotten that I committed a crime. I had forgotten the absolute reason behind this path I had chosen and had found a short cut to earn money. There was no stopping me. With no family to feed, no priorities or Goal in life, this life was the one I destined to. I was overwhelmed with it and decided to celebrate. That night at the hotel, I and my ego got drunk till I was knocked unconscious.

Next morning, I woke up with the sunlight. With nothing to do, I just laid on the bed, but didn't rest for long. I sat up and got back to exploring churches with easy exit and accessibility to transport. i.e., an autorickshaw or a cab.

I freshened up and walked across the town and then caught a cab to the nearby beach. It was still early morning, and I hoped the freshness in the air would help me fuel my thoughts. On my way back from the beach I got glimpse of a church on the other side of the road. I walked towards it and took a quick scan. Once I was satisfied, I marked this church as my next target. This was at Calangute, a city far away from my first heist and famous for the Calangute beach.

The next job involved eminent people, lots of security and yes, lots of money. This church was near the Calangute beach where a marriage ceremony was held that weekend. The notice board of the church had the details of the people getting married and I was shocked to learn it was the marriage of a movie star. Although I was feeling confident, I was scared. This was just my second job. I had tasted success at the first one but the second one didn't guarantee it. On the other hand, this wedding had to be huge. I expected at least three hundred people to participate. Rich people with rich movies stars, this was like a jackpot. My greed skyrocketed and I planned to steal more than one basket. It was difficult, but doable. I was eying thousands and by hook or by crook I had to get my hands on as many baskets as I could. I had five days to plan the perfect disguise and to smoothly execute the robbery. At such a high-class wedding nobody would even notice if few thousands were stolen and that's why I targeted small money at big churches.

I got busy collecting as much as information I could get about the bride and the groom and especially about the security. I found out that the bride and the groom were staying at a hotel near the beach. I knew about it as the entire hotel was booked for them and their guests and there were hundreds of paparazzi waiting outside to get a glimpse of the VIP's attending this wedding.

I wasn't sure if all of them would be at the church, but the count of guest's and their contribution surely would be a good one. But this information was of no use to me, I had to dig deep and so I decided to get friendly to one the of the keepers at the church, Mr. Gonzalo. Not as Johnny but disguised as a fifty-year-old Mr. D'Mello. That's right I wore a disguise of an old man to get friendly with Mr. Gonzalo.

It looked like Mr Gonzalo was into his fifties and had been a part of this church for many years. His interaction with people showed a compassionate side of his. He looked kind and down to earth. On the other hand, I was an evil genius and immediately attacked this simpleness of Mr. Gonzalo.

Mr. Gonzalo stayed alone in the quarters provided by the church located within the premises of the church. It was approximately fifteen feet from the church to the quarters. First thing I had to do, was to get close to Mr. Gonzalo, gain his confidence and then get him talking. Then started my five-day marathon.

Day -1 *started on a Monday evening at around five. Disguised as an old man, I walked into the church and sat on a bench staring at the altar. There was a sermon about to start. Mr. Gonzalo was helping the staff with the preparations when he saw me sitting alone on a bench in the corner of the church.*

I had doubts but I proved to be an excellent actor. It came naturally to me, and I was so deep into the character that anybody who saw or talked to me would never realize I was faking my age. My walk, seating style, body and jaw movement and the way of looking around was impeccable. At least that's what I thought.

I was acting as an old man troubled with life seeking God and was successful in displaying my helplessness and discontent which caught Mr. Gonzalos attention. He saw me with pity in his eyes and that was exactly what I had planned for. My plan had taken off as scripted.

Scene number one was perfect, and it was time to move on to next one. Then as it was time for the sermon, crowd started stepping in. Today, I hadn't planned on stealing anything and so I walked to the outside and sat under a tree...still in character. Then I heard the choir practicing their verses for the sermon. The band was playing beautifully, and the music was super catchy. This caught my attention and it pulled me back inside. I walked in to admire the musicians but was I was shocked to see that it wasn't a band but just one kid playing a piano and a guitar both at the same time. This kid wasn't more than sixteen years. I met this guy after the sermon and as I was still in the character, blessed him success. After witnessing the magic of music, I stepped outside the church and went back to the same spot under the tree where I sat till the sermon was over. I sat there for approximately two hours, but there was no sign of Mr. Gonzalo. He was busy cleaning up things post the sermon.

It was seven in the evening now and I was tired acting like an old man. My back was paining from the bending, my neck and jaw was paining from the constant movement and my buttock went numb after sitting for hours. It was time for me to get out of there before I gave away this false identity. Gently I got up, walked outside, took a cab and back to my place.

That evening with a drink in my hand I recollected what else could I do to improve my interaction with Mr. Gonzalo. Then I realized that in the evening may be because of daily sermons he would be busy before and after the sermon and the best time would be to meet him in the first half of the day. I even considered not getting involved with Mr. Gonzalo, but I needed the details of the marriage ceremony to make it a safe and a successful heist. That night with a glass of whiskey I watched a movie on television and in sometime was knocked out unconscious just like the night before.

Day -2 *- I got up at nine, had breakfast at the café and then came back to the room to change. To avoid any suspicion, I didn't change into disguise at this rented place instead I carried the toupee and the fake beard in a bag and wore it at a public restroom, at a less crowded gas station. I changed my look in the lavatory at a gas station. But I changed the location of the gas station to avoid looking suspicious to the ones monitoring the CCTV cameras which were covering the entry and exit.*

Then, I walked out to the next gas station. Stepped in the men's room as a young man and stepped out as an old man. I got back into the character and my walk, and body language changed. To add realism to the character, I bought a stick which supported my back and my character of an old helpless man.

Once everything was in place, I was on my way to the church in a cab and reached there in thirty minutes. From there I had to climb eighteen steps and then walk further towards the entrance, exactly ten steps more. Calculating the number of steps and the time taken to reach from point A to point B was extremely important as I was disguised as an old man and my walking speed needed to be constant. I memorized the distance and the steps the previous day.

It was twelve in the afternoon now when I reached the church. It was going be lunch time in another sixty minutes and hence I carried few snacks with me. There was no sermon going at this hour, but the church doors were open for people who came in to pray in silence. I walked in and sat at the same location as I did the day before hoping Mr Gonzalo would notice me, but Mr. Gonzalo wasn't around. Wasting time wasn't an option and so after sitting there for ten minutes I got up and strolled around. First inside and then outside the church.

First, I walked inside the church eyeballing every small thing. I didn't notice anything important apart from statues and photos of Jesus and Mother Mary and few burning candles on the stand. Then I noticed a door to another room. This was the room from where the priest entered before and exited post the sermon. Offertory money followed the priests into that room post every sermon. Surprisingly it was unlocked. I entered and saw it was a room full of shelves and cupboards and suspected them to be filled with valuables. Tried opening one of them, but it was locked. Just when I was about to touch another one, I heard footsteps. It was coming from where I had entered and hence running out the same direction was a bad idea. I was scared and shivering. This fear of getting caught, put an end to my acting and I came out of the character of the old man. I panicked and was ready to give up that's when I heard a voice "come this way". I turned around and it was Mr. Gonzalo standing behind me with an open door. There was a door behind one of the curtains which I missed. I immediately went along with Mr. Gonzalo. We both then peeked in from behind the curtain and it was the parish priest who walked in to check on few things. I breathed a sigh of relief and then accompanied Mr Gonzalo who invited me to his place.

I couldn't get back into the character knowing I was caught red handed, but I went with him anyways. When we reached his cottage, he offered me a drink. I didn't deny it but was a little sceptical to drink in a church premises.

"Take off this fake makeup" said Mr. Gonzalo and I did.

"How old are you" he asked, and I replied, "twenty-three".

"Why all of this" he asked but I was curious, and counter questioned, "how did you know I was faking".

Mr Gonzalo smiled, "I didn't till you sat here in front of me".

I was confused "what do you mean".

"I mean, first I thought you were lost, and I helped you because you weren't supposed to be in that room. The priest's hate people toiling in and around these rooms

and blames me for not stopping them" replied Mr Gonzalo.

I wasn't convinced and asked, "what gave me away".

Mr. Gonzalo replied, "Your beard, one side of your beard had come off".

I touched at it and felt my finger on my chin "OH! It must have come off during the panic attack I had in that room" I replied.

The situation tensed and there was awkward silence between us. I suspected something fishy was about to come up. This old guy was smart. He had finished his glass of whisky at one go while I was still sipping away.

"Why are you here and what do you intend to do? why disguised as an old man" Mr Gonzalo was straight to the point. I wasn't dumb either "I'm an actor and preparing for a role of an old man. I have an audition coming up in the next week, preparing for that".

This wasn't the best but still an acceptable response.

Again, there was silence. None of us uttered a word and stared right into each other's eyes. There was aggression in Mr Gonzalo's eyes which scared me. I anticipated this situation to get physical and was ready for it. I had already spotted potential weapons in the room which I could use to fight Mr. Gonzalo and I even had one in my hands, the glass of whisky. Mr. Gonzalo did the same thing. He too was ready to fight and looked around for a weapon to fight. Suddenly Mr. Gonzalo snorted loudly and laughed. At first, I didn't understand but then I couldn't control and joined him. We both started laughing. Then we both stopped.

Mr Gonzalo said, "let's start again. I know you have cruel intentions, and I don't buy the crap about acting. You came back here looking for something and only thing that you can find in a church is either money or expensive statues and paintings. Now, I have been here since years and don't see any expensive statues and paintings so that leaves us 'Money'. Who told you there is money in this church"? responded Mr Gonzalo.

I was stunned by what Mr Gonzalo had said but as I was a disbeliever of God, an atheist, I didn't agree to what Mr. Gonzalo said.

"No money here? What are you saying? till the time there are God fearing people in the world churches and temples will be poured in with money" he replied.

"Okay, now that I know, you came here to steal, I will give you two options. One, handover you to the cops and two, you let me in on whatever you are planning to steal" replied Mr. Gonzalo and added, "I have been a caretaker of this church for almost ten years now, I have seen people come and go and even Priests for that matter and none of them have done anything for me. I have lived my life a poor man and don't intent to die that way. I don't care anymore about these selfish people. So, whatever it is, I'm in."

I didn't expect this response. I was new at this and had hard time trusting people. I was at my best when I went solo. On the other hand, Mr. Gonzalo was the inside man I needed and could help me in making this heist a success. Mr. Gonzalo was the key here but to the outside world he was just a dead weight and then there was also a possibility that Mr Gonzalo might double cross me. How could I trust a man who after so many years turned his back to God? I was confused and running out of options. Then despite all the negative thoughts, I decided to partner with Mr. Gonzalo. After all my cover was exposed by him.

"Okay, but I will dictate the terms and I need an assurance that you won't backstab me" I laid this condition and Mr. Gonzalo nodded yes.

"There is a big dream wedding planned this weekend and I'm planning to steal the money that will be collected during the sermon. If I'm not wrong, it should easily be somewhere around twenty to thirty thousand" I disclosed my plan to Mr. Gonzalo but didn't get the reaction that I was hoping for.

"That's it! this is your plan. You plan to steal the offertory money?" Mr. Gonzalo responded, and this time I nodded 'Yes'.

"All of these efforts just for few thousand bucks?" Mr. Gonzalo responded, and I nodded 'Yes'.

"I'm having second thoughts about associating with you now".

There was something cooking in Mr Gonzalos mind, and I sensed it. Why wasn't this a big deal for him when it's a gigantic one for me. I was eager to know what Mr. Gonzalo had in mind and so i asked "Why? What do you have in mind?"

Mr Gonzalo looked at me, walked towards me and grabbed me by my hands and took me outside.

"Look at it, see how big this church is. There are thousand family's part of this parish and all of them loaded with money. Every week the amount generated from the offertory collections and the donations crosses lakhs of rupees, and you plan to steal few thousands. It won't make any difference. Nobody would even notice it."

"Nobody would notice. That is what I want, if nobody would notice there wouldn't be any enquiry" I replied.

"Son! how long do you plan on stealing drops of water from the ocean? go for a big one and then you don't have to do anything like this again." Mr. Gonzalo made a valid point.

This was experience speaking and it made sense. I was silenced by what Mr. Gonzalo's said. I realized I couldn't go on forever stealing small bucks. I had to get my hands on something big which would take care of my future. This thought followed me my life. I guess my mind wasn't satisfied with what I was doing and hence forced me to jump into new things.

"What do you have in mind" I asked him.

"Not here son. We meet outside to talk about it, but not today. Go home and meet me at the beach tomorrow at the same time," said Mr Gonzalo. Then as he turned around to go back to his room I asked, "Is this your first time?" Mr. Gonzalo turned smiled around and walked away. This evil smile said a lot about Mr Gonzalo.

It was a power packed discussion, and I was still experiencing the adrenaline. On my way back, I kept thinking about Mr. Gonzalo. There were lots of questions that needed answers, especially about the background of Mr. Gonzalo. I was now eager to discover who Mr. Gonzalo was and what was his story. But it was almost impossible to know about someone's life without stalking them or taking help from the cops. I faced this difficulty too. I wasn't sure how and where to start and if I could trust Mr. Gonzalo. I was again in two minds and again had two options. First one whether to go with Mr. Gonzalo or not and second one to forget everything and hunt for a new place. After all I didn't give Mr. Gonzalo anything which could be traceable, not even my name. But the greed of becoming rich had blinded me and after all Mr Gonzalo had ignited this fire in me. So, I decided to meet Mr. Gonzalo the next day and face whatever was in store for me.

After the conversation with Mr. Gonzalo, I left the church but didn't go back to the rented room. Instead, I went to the nearby theatre to watch a movie. As you know, I am crazy for movies and hadn't been to one since long. The movie chose to see that day was "The Saint" a movie about a thief expert in wearing disguises and that's why I chose to watch it and still remember it in bits and pieces. I collected as many ideas as I could from that movie. After all I had become a thief myself.

While watching "The Saint" I came up with an idea to secretly keep an eye on Mr. Gonzalo. To know the old man's moves and to test his loyalty towards me. After the movie, I visited a wig maker and bought few more hairpieces, moustaches, and beards. I also bought new clothes and changed into a new look.

Then took a cab and went back to the church. It was six in the evening. This time I wasn't an old man, but a young guy wearing a cap, a moustache, a beard, and pair of glasses.

There was no sermon today and hence the church wasn't crowded. There were hardly ten to fifteen people who had come to pray. As soon as I reached the church, I went in search of Mr. Gonzalo who was sitting on a bench looking at the huge statue of Jesus Christ in front at the altar. Maybe he was confessing his sins which he was about to commit.

I sat two rows behind Mr. Gonzalo from where I had a good view of the entire hall. There was no movement from Mr. Gonzalo like he was statue, and this continued for the next fifteen minutes. It was difficult to tell from behind if Mr. Gonzalo was alive or dead. He didn't move at all. This scared me for a moment but then the parish priest showed up wearing shorts and a t-shirt and called for Mr Gonzalo. They both went into that room where I was hiding the previous day. I followed them and peeked from behind the curtain. They were arguing about something.

The priest then opened one of the cupboards, picked up something which was wrapped in a plastic bag and threw it to Mr. Gonzalo. Then the priest locked the cupboard and left from the back door while Mr. Gonzalo stood there for some more time and then followed the priest outside. I followed them the same way. The priest went back into his office and Mr. Gonzalo to his room. I followed Mr Gonzalo.

Mr. Gonzalo went back to his cottage where I followed and peeked inside through the gap in the window panel to see what was going on. I saw Mr. Gonzalo lying on the bed with the plastic bag next to him which wasn't opened yet. Mr. Gonzalo was again like a statue. He didn't move for another ten minutes. At that moment I wandered how could a person be so still for such a long time. Being immovable like a statue was a rare superpower of Mr Gonzalo. I got restless seeing Mr. Gonzalo just lying there. But then, Mr Gonzalo moved. He got up and walked towards the washroom. He carried the bag with him, but then he came back to bed and emptied the bag on the bed. Down fell bundles of money, three of them. I was shocked. 'What the hell was going on? why did the parish priest pay so much money to Mr. Gonzalo? I was suspicious and needed answers.

Mr. Gonzalo didn't even count it. He put the money back in the bag then walked towards the mirror on the wall and stared at it. He stared straight for ten minutes and again without any damn movement. This so-called 'being a statue' frustrated me. Then he moved, pulled down the mirror and on the backside of the mirror was a brown patch. He pushed the patch up from one side and down fell a key. Picking up the key he walked back towards the bed and stood on the bed for couple of seconds, then got down. From the corner of the room, he picked up a small ladder, stood on it and pulled down the big panel holding the three tube lights. Then the lights went off. It was seven in the evening and the entire room was covered with darkness. I couldn't see anything, and Mr Gonzalo couldn't either. Then, 'thud' there was a huge noise, and I was sure Mr. Gonzalo experienced the force of gravity on his ass. It was still dark, and I just kept guessing what was happening inside. I was sure that whatever Mr. Gonzalo was doing was stupid and that confused me.

Then I heard Mr. Gonzalo panting, pulling himself up and after some time the lights came on. The panel and the tube lights were back at their position and the bag disappeared. He then laid back on the bed and maybe he slept. I knew Mr Gonzalo was strange but what I saw that day was out of the ordinary. 'Where did the bag go? Why would Mr. Gonzalo take off a working light panel? I said to myself and was dead set on finding it out.

That evening I went back to my place and as usual had drinks, lots of it. I kept thinking about the incident back at the church and suspected something was horribly wrong. There was more to the story of   Mr. Gonzalo which I needed to explore. Then with the rigorous thinking, my intake of alcohol increased and for the third night in a row, I was knocked out unconscious. But that night was different. That night I had peed my pants. I was tired and so deep in sleep that even the wetness didn't wake me up.

Day -3 - *Next morning I woke up at the same time as I did the day before and immediately looked down at my pants. Pants were dry but I could still smell the urine. I felt embarrassed but with nobody around I* *cared less and freshened up. I am mentioning this to you to tell you I don't do that anymore. Then I had breakfast at the same time, at the same café, at the same table and went back to my room. I had timed these daily activities just in case and it took me exactly forty-three minutes to finish freshening up and the breakfast. "Timing every activity" was something I took from the movies. It wasn't useful all the time, but it gave me the feeling of thinking like a 'Spy.*

Still shaken from what I had seen that evening at the church, I was again in two minds whether to meet Mr. Gonzalo or to forget everything and start new. This was the third time I had reconsidered my alliance with Mr Gonzalo. But I had seen something that day that my mastermind demanded to get to the root of. I was convinced that Mr. Gonzalo had a secret and was definitely hiding something. The fight with the parish priest, the climbing up on the bed and then taking off the lights, this wasn't an act of stupidity. It was obvious, there was something behind the light panels. Mr. Gonzalo was weird but surely not stupid.

That day I didn't wear disguise. Mr. Gonzalo had already seen my face. So, at eleven I called a cab and was on my way. I reached the church's gate within thirty minutes and walked inside the church. I looked everywhere but couldn't find Mr Gonzalo. Rather than waiting at the church I decided to go for a walk at the beach which was twenty minutes from the church. I had been to this church few times but today was the first time I saw the beach up close. It was a beautiful beach. It was the month of May, and the beach was sky blue in colour with waves as high as six feet. As it was the holiday season, the beach was crowded with tourists and the noise was ear-splitting.

I strolled on the beach for some time. Then at the opposite corner I was surprised to see Mr Gonzalo and he was holding an umbrella for a lady who was lying on the beach in her bikini. She wasn't Indian may be British. This was weird to see but then it was Mr. Gonzalo. May be this act was another way of redeeming himself for the bad things that he had done in his life.

I hid behind a boat which was anchored to the shore and watched Mr Gonzalo. I wanted to see what was going on. Not to mention Mr Gonzalo stood there 'without any movement' looking like an actual beach umbrella. I wondered if that lady even knew that a human was holding this umbrella. Then the girl rolled over and said something to Mr. Gonzalo. He then closed the umbrella, kept it aside, sat down and loosened the girl's bikini. Then Mr. Gonzalo stood there while the girl soaked in the sun.

An old man at the mercy of a young half naked women was too disturbing to see. I then walked towards Mr. Gonzalo and once our eyes met, I signalled him to meet me at the corner behind another boat on the other side. Mr. Gonzalo denied. He had to help this lady get back to wherever she came from.

It was thirty minutes now and I realized the girl didn't move. It was impossible to lay with a naked back on this hot sunny day, but she did. Then she moved, wrapped herself in a towel and started walking out. Mr Gonzalo carried her bags and escorted her while I kept waiting. May be this was one more reason for Mr Gonzalos "Job dissatisfaction".

Our meeting was scheduled to start at twelve and it was around one now. Sun was on my head, and it was insanely hot. There was no shade out on the beach where I could take cover. So, to cool off I went to the nearby hotel ordered beer and snacks and waited for Mr Gonzalo. I still had twelve hundred bucks left with me and planned on spending only two hundred.

An hour had passed. There was no sign of Mr. Gonzalo. The longer I waited the more beers I had and till four in the evening, I was five beers down. I had crossed the budget that I had set for the day. Finally, after completing the sixth beer I gave up. I paid the bill and walked out of the hotel towards the church to check up on Mr. Gonzalo. I went straight to the cottage and peeked in from the same gap in the window. Mr. Gonzalo was lying on the bed with his eyes closed. I assumed Mr Gonzalo was tired from standing in the super-hot sun carrying an umbrella and was sleeping.

I gently stepped inside from the half-opened door and intended on finding out the secret about the key which was bothering me. I first checked up on Mr Gonzalo who was unconscious than in sleep. Then just like Mr. Gonzalo did the day before I approached the mirror, stared at it, and laughed at Mr. Gonzalo who was lying on the bed. I then took down the mirror and turned it around hoping to find the key that I saw Mr. Gonzalo reach out to the previous day, but there was nothing there. No panel no key nothing. Out of frustration I approached Mr. Gonzalo and gently gave him a little push to wake him up, but he didn't move. I did it couple of times more and then as there was no response, I kicked him on his butt. Mr. Gonzalo didn't move. I then checked his breath and Mr Gonzalo wasn't breathing. There were no pulse or heartbeat either. I realized, Mr Gonzalo was dead, and this passed a shiver through me, and I just stood there in shock, like a statue, like Mr Gonzalo. This was something I hadn't expected or wished to happen. To confirm if he was really dead, I gave him a little shake couple of times. I also gave him mouth to mouth CPR but couldn't continue as his mouth stank. Now I was convinced that Mr. Gonzalo was dead and so were my hopes of something big.

I realized that staying there was dangerous and immediately ran out of the room away from the dead body. Informing others about Mr. Gonzalo's death crossed my mind but then it would be too much of enquires on me and that was the last thing I wanted. I knew someone would surely come looking and will find him. So, I sticked to my plan of running away from the crime scene. I had to make sure nobody saw me walking out of the church and I gently managed to get pass the couple of people who had come to pray and the security cameras covering the exits of the church. Once outside the church premise, I immediately caught a cab and took off.

Shaken by the death of Mr. Gonzalo, I didn't go back to the hotel. Instead, I went to another beach. I still had few hundred with me and bought bears. It was now eight in the evening, and I had plan to drown myself in alcohol like my chances of getting rich had drowned. The beach was far from the church and was almost empty. The only people left at the beach were either alcoholics or drug addicts.

I didn't realize but they all were hiding at different corners of the shore, and I was the only one in front and in the centre of the shore. I wasn't sure what they were hiding from, drinking on beaches was legal in Goa and so I carried on. I was already high with all the alcohol when I realized certain disturbance in this silent night. I couldn't see clearly, but I heard noises and saw few people running across the shore. At first, I thought it was a Tsunami and people were running around saving themselves. For a normal person the thought of drowning in a Tsunami would set him sprinting away but not me. That day I wasn't an ordinary man who was scared to die. I planned on drowning in alcohol not in a Tsunami. So, I laid there surrendering my life to it. But unfortunately, it wasn't the huge splash of the waves I expected instead it was smack of a wooden stick right on my back. It was an attack by the local cops.

I was so high that I didn't even realize what was happening and instantly reacted and my reaction made things worse for me that night. My reaction included two punches, one to the face and another one right in the middle of a fat belly and the unlucky recipient was one of the two cops.

Things changed with a blink of an eye. Just moments ago, I was lying on the beach in peace thinking about Mr Gonzalo and mourning not the death of Mr

Gonzalo but the death of my hopes of getting rich. And now I was in the back of a police van alongwith few other drug addicts. Few of them high fiving each other like they were long lost friends going on a trip. I avoided eye contact with them and was a little scared. Still high from the drinking I didn't have a clear vision either and so I closed my eyes to relax and in some time I slept.

Day 4 *– It was past twelve now and in sometime the van stopped. I was woken up by the sudden noise of people talking to each other. I thought it was the station and I got up to get down, but it wasn't the police station instead the van had stopped in the middle of nowhere. I glanced outside the window, and it was dark. Nothing was visible. I leaned and looked over the driver's shoulder and saw a long road ahead. It was clear and lightened up by the front lights of the Van.*

"What the fuck you think you are doing, sit down" the cop yelled at me, and I sat back.

Nobody spoke in the van and the cops signalled each other about something. Now this scared me. I had seen such horrifying situations in the movies where the cops stop the van, everyone gets down and then the cops shoot the ones arrested, it's called "Encounter". Here too the van had stopped but nobody got down instead one cop from the driver's side-stepped in. He was a tall guy with the physique of Hercules. Guys like him controlled every place they went. He was the main guy and commanded everyone in the van to get up. The guy then asked everyone to pay him money. It wasn't surprising at all. A group of corrupt cop's demanding money. Ten were arrested from the beach including me and the ones who paid were let go. Everyone had to pay and after the seventh one paid and stepped out it was my turn. There were three of us left.

I assumed I had some cash left from the latest alcohol purchase but when I went through my pockets, it was empty. My wallet was gone. I was absolutely sure I had money on me but had no clue why my pockets were empty. I realized this was going to be a long night to remember.

Everyone handed money to the Herculean guy and now i was asked to approach.

"I've got nothing, no money, no hope nothing" I said to the main guy. The main guy looked at me with fire in his eyes. There was a beast about to unleash on me and that's when I was struck with a blazing fist. This punch was so strong that I collapsed and felt few of my teeth cracking. This guy was a powerful fellow with a punching velocity easily above a normal human being. Flinging my hands, I tried to pull myself up. But then the cop whom I had thrown couple of punches, took this moment to get back to me. This was his time for payback and this crazy cop went crazy on me. Kicks after kicks, I took it all without fighting back. That's when my life flashed in front of my eyes. I saw death in the form of these cops and promised myself never to be at the mercy of cops anymore. This beating that I took from the cops made me stronger. Other ruthless cops stood there watching. Then one of the arrested

guys couldn't take it. He requested the leader to stop this onslaught on me and in return agreed to pay my share. Once the payment was done this guy helped me get up and then carried me out of the van. Once everyone had paid these corrupt cops the van left the sight.

All the arrested ones walked away while me and this guy sat there at the side of the road.

"Thanks for saving my ass," I said to him wiping the blood off my mouth.

"You're welcome, bro" replied this guy and added "Hi, I'm Romeo".

We introduced ourselves shaking hands.

"Here, take it, this belongs to you I suppose", Romeo handed me something which wasn't clear in the dark. I took it and it was my wallet which I thought was lost.

"I took it from you when you were snoozing," said Romeo.

"You had it with you all this time? you realize that if I had paid them first-hand, they would have left me unharmed, spared me the beating" I said to him in disbelief. Romeo acknowledged, apologized, and said, "Then we wouldn't have met."

I was mad at him, but I wasn't angry anymore and I smiled. I liked Romeo. He seemed like a good guy.

"Now what" I asked him.

"Either we walk or get a lift out of here" replied Romeo as he took a cigarette out of his pocket and lit a smoke.

This Romeo character was quirky one and I realized it when he refused to share a cigarette with me. Nobody does that after going through all of this. It was like kicking a man when he was down.

It was now four in the morning. Waiting there for a lift was stupid thing to do and so we choose a direction and walked. We both weren't sure if we were going to the city or out of it but went with our instinct.

"Why were you at the beach all alone" asked Romeo.

"I could ask you the same thing" I replied.

"I wasn't alone, my friends ran away when they saw the cops coming" replied Romeo.

"Why didn't you run" I asked.

"I wasn't finished" replied Romeo.

"Finished what?" I asked.

"Taking a dump" Romeo responded cheerfully.

I had a clue that Romeo was talking about potty but his cheerful response confused me and so I asked, "were you caught by the cops while you were doing potty?".

"Potty! what are you a child? but yes".

"At the beach" Romeo nodded 'yes' I further asked, *"did u at least finish and where did u wash?"*

"Well... It stopped instantly when this cop stood right in front of me, and yes, he did allow me to wash. In fact,

he was a good man he even offered me water you know... to wash".

This was a bizarre little conversation that ended with both of us laughing. We laughed so loud that the noise of it echoed in this silent dark night. We both were strangers but felt a connection, felt like we knew each other a long time. This little incident, this little moment was the beginning of a new friendship which would go on...at least I thought so.

"There is a saying, 'one can find love in weirdest of places, same goes with finding a friend and there couldn't be a place weirder than a police van" I said to Romeo, and he nodded "yeah!'.

We were now walking for about thirty minutes and there was no sign of any vehicle coming for our rescue. Thirty minutes turned into an hour. Last twenty-four were the worst ones for me and it had debilitated me. Every step I took I felt the pain in my feet and other parts of the body. I was without any food or water for more than six hours now and was worn out with all the beating I took. After walking for some time, I collapsed. I woke up with the first ray of sunlight and Romeo was gone, again with my money. That was the end of our so called "Friendship" which lasted only for hours.

When I opened my eyes, I was still dehydrated with all the beating and the intake of alcohol and could barely pick myself up. First attempt to lift myself failed miserably and I immediately fell flat on the ground. Then, I remembered last night's beating at the hands of the cops and that gave me the extra boost of energy that I needed. I got up the second time and dusted myself. My shirt was torn at multiple places, and it had taken the colour of mud I was lying in all night and to top it up, I had no money. While I wanted to get back to Romeo for stealing from me and throwing me away like garbage, he wasn't the priority. The priority was to get out of here and to get back to my hotel room as early as possible.

Hoping to find lift, I chose a direction and followed it. Luckily in about twenty minutes, I heard a car approaching my way. This was my chance to get out of there and I had to make it count. I immediately took out my right thumb and asked for a lift. It was a truck, and the truck drivers are known for their generosity in helping the hikers and this one was no different. The truck stopped for me. I climbed onto the backside of the truck, and we drove off.

In an hour I was dropped off to the nearby bus station from where it was another one hour walk back to the hotel room. I knew it and suddenly felt an energy rush my body which helped me drag myself to the hotel and in some time I reached. I slipped in gently through the reception area and went towards my room. But this wasn't the end of my misery. I had lost the only key I had. After such a horrendous twenty-four hours all I wanted was to take calming hot bath and something to eat but I had to wait.

With no options left I approached the reception and asked for the spare key. The lady at the reception refused me straight away and asked me for evidence that I had rented this room. I had nothing on me, and I tried convincing her but failed. I even told the lady that I went out for couple of drinks and ended up having more, tried to summarize my appearance but it didn't change that stubborn lady's mind who kept on arguing. Then came the rescuer, "The Manager". The manager was a guy in his thirties and understood me. He immediately gave me the spare key saying, "What happens in Goa stays in Goa right". I smiled and acknowledged. Then went back to my room while the lady stared at the manager with anger in her eyes. "Relax, we all were young once and have done something stupid". The manager said to the lady and got back to work.

As soon as I entered the room, I ran to the bathroom and drowned myself into the bathtub. I laid there for some time and then got up, got ready and got something to eat.

It was now eleven and a funeral for Mr. Gonzalo was held at the church. I was aware of it and wanted to offer my condolences. So, after freshening up I was on my way to the church. This time I went in as myself with no disguises and in some time, I reached the church.

There were many people gathered for the funeral and it felt good to see Mr Gonzalo getting a well-deserved goodbye. Funerals made me extremely emotional and sad and even though I wasn't related to Mr. Gonzalo, seeing him dead brought tears to my eyes. It reminded me of my mother's funeral.

Mr. Gonzalo's body was kept in a coffin placed inside the church just below the alter and there were people sharing their tribute as a way of respect. Even the

British lady soaking in the sun on the beach showed up. First, the priest spoke about Mr Gonzalo and then he called up his family. An old lady got up maybe she was his wife and then came the son. I didn't know Mr Gonzalo's family but was super surprised to see that Mr Gonzalo's son was Romeo. That's right the one i had spent last night with. My short time friend who left me to die at the mercy of the night. Once the old lady paid her tribute, came the prodigal son. I was eagerly waiting to hear what he had to say and to everyone's surprise Romeo started off with a Joke.

"Knock, Knock" he said and looked at the crowd with a weird smile. Nobody responded, everyone at the funeral was stunned. Romeo asked again, "Knock, Knock" and this time someone responded, "who's there?" and this someone was Me. Romeo's face lit up when he saw me and added, "He's gone", I asked, "who?", "Daddy's gone without leaving anything for me" Romeo was still high and further added, "I am telling you a joke and the only thing to remember at a funeral are the jokes, you know why? because they never die" and started laughing.

Romeo wasn't in the right state of mind, and this was nothing but insult to the dead man. All the people were silent to the rubbish that Romeo uttered. Even the priest had seen enough and so guided Romeo down from the alter and proceeded with the ceremony. Once the ceremony was complete with all the tributes and the formalities, Mr. Gonzalo was buried in the graveyard behind this church where he spent most of his years serving God.

Few minutes earlier Romeo acted like a jerk and disrespected his dad, but he was still there at the graveyard till everyone left and was in tears. He missed his dad and couldn't control himself. I stood beside him, held him reassuring everything was going to be fine.

After an hour all the people started going back to their normal lives and it was only me and Romeo left. Romeo's overflowing dam of tears had stopped, and he was just sitting there looking at his dad's tombstone.

"You know, he was never really there for me or my family. He is the reason my family fell apart. I hated him for what he did, and I never forgave him for that. I can never go back in time or right the wrong but If I'm given another chance, I would surely hope that things were better than how they ended between us" said Romeo bowing his head at the tombstone.

"This is the shit called 'life' and there is nothing you can do to control it. I blame God for what I'm today and you blame your dad. We both are sailing in the same boat bro. let's go. At least your mom is here, take care of her" I replied.

"My mom, nope…she is not my mom. She is my dad's affair. She is the reason why my mom and dad separated. My mother passed away couple of years ago and since then I haven't spoken to him. See even though my dad served god for the remainder of his life, he wasn't a saint" saying this Romeo got up.

"Maybe he realized what he did was wrong and serving God was his way of repenting" I added.

"Dude you don't know my dad, he will never do anything for anyone, unless there is something in it for him" said Romeo as he walked away.

I gulped down his thoughts and hid the fact that I had spoken to Mr. Gonzalo in the last few days and that I was there when Mr. Gonzalo took his last breath. I wasn't sure if I could trust Romeo but agreed to what he said about his dad. Mr. Gonzalo had something going on in this church and even I had witnessed a glimpse of it, but what was it? and should I tell Romeo about it?

In all this rush of things, I hadn't forgotten about the destination wedding that was about to take place at this church in twenty-four hours. This was the jackpot I've been waiting for four days. Time was of the essence now and so I had to rush back. I waved goodbye to Romeo who was walking away lost in his own world.

In the absence of Mr Gonzalo, I now had to plan the entry and exit from the church post heist which was Mr Gonzalo's responsibility. I needed to spend time in there and had to do it at the speed of light. Reason being the church was getting decorated for the marriage and in few hours' entry to most part of the church would be prohibited.

My plan was to steal the money collected during the sermon, but Mr. Gonzalo had something else in mind. This thought haunted me, but I couldn't figure out the *missing piece. It was like the key to unlock this mystery died with him. On second thought I knew that the best place where I could find any clue was at the cottage where Mr. Gonzalo stayed. So, against my own will I decided to go back to the crime scene.*

I reached the cottage and surprisingly there was nobody there. It wasn't even locked which was strange. Mr Gonzalo was dead on that bed making this room a crime scene, but this didn't look like one. While I stood there in disbelief, I heard someone speak, "were you close to him" I said 'No' and turned around. Standing there was the priest and Romeo.

"What are you doing here and how do you know my dad" asked Romeo.

"I didn't" I replied with a scary look.

"Why are you attending his funeral If you didn't know him" asked Romeo suspecting something was wrong.

"I stay nearby and come to beach very often. While I was at the beach, I heard about this funeral. I've never been to a funeral before and thought why not witness it today"

"Son, nobody comes to this part of the church. How and why did you?" asked the priest.

I knew I was in trouble, "Well Funeral was one thing and secondly I was trying to explore this beautiful church. This is an awesome place. I stepped in here as the gate was open. Maybe the people decorating this place left it open."

This wasn't a satisfactory response and Romeo suspected something fishy.

"But there is no decoration here nobody has been here what are you talking about?" replied the priest.

The priest then asked me to get out of there before he called the cops and immediately, I marched away. But I wasn't even out of the church when Romeo came calling.

"Dude you are a man full of secrets. At first you wander around alone on the beach in the middle of the night and then you come here. What are you up to?" asked Romeo.

Romeo had a lava of questions boiling inside him about to erupt. I thought if I talked about it to Romeo, maybe Romeo could help. So, I decided to tell him everything about the conversation that I had with his father. It was also a burden which I had to get off my chest. There was one problem though, just like Mr. Gonzalo, I didn't trust Romeo, but I was running out of options. I had a plan, a plan to break open this suspense and get the hell out of here with lots of money, if there was any. I was still angry from the last nights betrayal of trust, but I didn't bring it up.

"Come with me" I took him to the beach.

"I don't care if you trust me or not. I don't care if you go and tell anyone what I'm about to tell you" I started off with a threat. "Let me tell you something about your dad. I met him here at this church about a week ago. Sorry, let me start again. I was spying on your dad *trying to know him. He had something that I was dying to get my hands on".*

Romeo was confused. "Why were you spying on my old man? and what did he have that you wanted. He was a quaint man staying in a cottage provided by the church. What did he possibly have that interested you?"

Now was the time to disclose his dads' cruel intentions to Romeo.

"I will tell you but promise not to tell anyone." I needed one more nod of confirmation from Romeo which I got. It was a risk, but I went with it anyway.

"I'm an offertory thief," I said.

"What is an offertory thief?" asked confused Romeo.

"I steal offertory money" I replied, and Romeo laughed.

"You do what? Hearing something weird like this for the first-time bro. Who would be crazy enough to steal an offertory and how much can he earn from it compared to the risks involved"?

Whatever Romeo said made sense. But I was brainwashed and blinded by the guilt. I convinced Romeo that stealing offertory money was indeed a cool thing to do.

"Okay I agree. You are cool and stealing offertory money is also cool. But what did that have to do with my father. What was it that you wanted from him? By the way how did you meet?" responded Romeo and this time he had his hands on my shoulder. This was a

move showing who was dominating whom, but I wasn't scared. I shoved his hands off and stood right in front of him.

"Listen, I will eventually get there" I replied and started telling Romeo the story of his life. I don't know why but I told him everything. About the death of my parents, how my friends and my girlfriend parted ways and how I ran out of Mumbai and slumped in Goa. I also added the time I spent staying with the wasted drug addicts at my previous job. Then came the part when I needed money to get a decent look for an interview and to go back home to Mumbai to get my documents. I was so into the story that I told Romeo about my first successful attempt at stealing the offertory and the greed that possessed me to steal more.

Romeo who was stunned in silence.

"Why didn't you just go back home and lived a normal life, like a freaking normal person?" asked Romeo. I ignored him and carried on with the story. Eventually came the part where I found this church and found Mr. Gonzalo. I told Romeo about the argument between Mr. Gonzalo and the parish priest. I also talked about the multiple suspicious cupboards in the room behind the alter and the mysterious roof in the cottage where Mr. Gonzalo stayed.

For Romeo this was stupid and too good to be true. "You watch lot of movies or what? these things happen only in the movies," said Romeo.

"Dude, I have seen it with my own eyes, it's your call to believe it or not. And one more thing, …your dad told me once that he didn't care about these selfish people or God and wanted to be part of what I was planning. Think about it and let me know when you are ready for a discussion. It's not only about stealing the offertory money but there's something huge".

My words in a patrician tone left Romeo thinking and I knew I said enough for Romeo to come back and guess what he did. Like me, Romeo's greed wouldn't let it go and then things got exciting.

Romeo wanted to know more about my plan, and I told him the remaining part about Mr. Gonzalo's secret cottage where I suspected money was hidden.

"In my dad's cottage? Not possible. I know my dad bro if he had lots of money like you mentioned why would he still stay here?" asked Romeo.

He had a point, and this is where I was left hanging by the sudden death of Mr. Gonzalo.

"Yes, I ask myself the same question, but I think he must have got that money just recently. You know there is a destination wedding being held here tomorrow. Maybe that has some connection to it. let's look for it. If we don't find anything, we got nothing to lose, but if we do find something we share and then part our ways".

This time I was precise, and Romeo agreed. We turned back and hiding away from the parish priest stepped into the cottage.

"This is where he entered with the bag of money" I said nearing the mirror on the wall. *"He took this mirror down and here was a key".* But even today the panel behind the mirror was empty. *"We need to find that key, it's the only thing that can unveil the mystery,"* I said, and Romeo wasn't convinced.

"Tell me one thing, you said he took the key from behind this mirror right" asked Romeo.

"yes" I replied while searching the key in the room.

"He did what, what was his next move?" asked curious Romeo.

"Well, he climbed on this bed pulled down the light and… I didn't see what he did after that," I replied.

"Okay so this light panel is the key here. I have one question though, why do you need a key when you can pull down the panel" asked Romeo. I realized it was a simple task, but it hadn't crossed his mind.

"you're right, I never thought of it" saying this I jumped on the bed and pulled down the light panel. Behind the panel was a small metal box. It was like a safe. *"I guess this is why we need the key,"* I said.

"No, we don't," said Romeo.

Then he climbed up on the bed and broke the plaster around the box. As the plaster around the box loosened it came off. But alongwith the box came down a major part of the roof and few more boxes that were hidden in there. Romeo picked up one of them and banged it on the floor to open it.

"Here take your wallet back you might need it now" Romeo gave me my wallet back and we both smiled. This was the third time it had happened.

From the box, peeked out bundle of money. There were eight boxes more and we hoped it was filled with money too. Immediately we grabbed them and snuck them in our clothes and sprinted out of the church.

It was afternoon and there were people at every corner. We couldn't take the risk of opening all the boxes here and so had to get away from the people. We went to the nearby restaurant and rented a room. This was Goa but still India. Two guys hiring a room raised eyebrows. The receptionist looked at us like we were a couple and happily handed us a room with a beach facing view.

We both walked into the room and locked it from inside. Then got to opening the boxes. One was already opened at the crime scene and eight were remaining. The one box which was opened at the cottage had three bundles of hundred rupees notes and each bundle contained ten thousand rupees. Seven out of the eight boxes had money in them. Same as the first box. Three bundles of hundred rupees and the last one had couple of diamond rings. Maybe it was of the bride and the groom who were to marry in twenty-four hours. Then we counted the money and each box contained thirty thousand bucks which was two lakhs forty thousand rupees in total. This changed everything. Our plan to steal offertory money disappeared like melting snow in springtime and a whole new scene was created.

This was huge like Mr. Gonzalo mentioned and too much for us to handle. But keeping our cool we decided to equally distribute the money and then part their ways. Once the money was distributed, the distribution of the rings was a tough one. Mathematically it was simple two rings and two people but tough because I wasn't in the favour of stealing them. I am a staunch supporter of marriage and wanted to give these rings back to the bride and the groom. It was their wedding day, and I wasn't planning on ruining it. I had already stolen money from them.

Romeo wasn't in favour of returning the rings. It was diamond which meant more money and giving the rings back involved risk of getting caught. Secondly, Romeo wasn't planning on going back to the church ever again. We argued about it but then I gave him couple of bundles from my share of the money which Romeo agreed to take and then walked out of the room. As agreed earlier, we both parted ways and I went straight back to my hotel room. This night was my last night here and I had to check out in the morning.

I had the most exciting, most thrilling and the most dangerous twenty-four hours one could imagine. I went from almost being a prime suspect in Mr Gonzalo's death to spending time in jail to almost getting killed in the night and then getting my hands on lakhs of rupees. This wasn't easy money though, I had to earn it. May be the wrong way but I had earned it. If something like this happens to a normal person his perception of the Gods belief would change. He would fall head over heels and praise the lord but not me.

Instead, this was somewhat a demeaning victory for me.

That night for the first time I ordered room service full of exotic and special dishes and upgraded myself to a costlier brand of whisky. Then as usual I drank to sleep. But was woken up many times as I was concerned about the money.

Day 5 - *God created the world in six days and rested on the seventh. I strategized this moment for four days and on the fifth day, after a lot of hard and smart work, got what I had set out to do. I had no reason to go back to this church. I should have been enjoying the stealing's, but I had only one thing on my mind. To give back the rings to the rightful owners. You see, this was a pure thought of good deed but also stupid. No robber would risk going back to the crime scene and that too within twenty-four hours. I knew It was a ridiculous idea to go back to the place where I stole the money from and where the priest had seen my face.*

That morning I got up at seven and first thing I did was count the money. I had hidden it under the mattress and was concerned about its safety all night. Once I was finished counting the money, I wrapped it up in a bag and hid it in the cabinet and got to freshen up. As always, my plan was to walk into the church in disguise and seek for the perfect moment to swoop in and hand back the rings. Again, I agree that on paper this was a good crude plan but in reality, this was foolish on multiple levels.

This was going to be my last visit to this church, and I wanted to make it memorable. Not to forget the fact that I was walking into a lion's den, to top it up, I decided to take photos with the staff of the church including the parish priests. There was one problem though, my bag of cosmetic had nothing new. I had already worn the available disguises earlier and didn't get a good feeling to go with it again. So, today, I came up with a new-fangled look, something different from all my earlier disguises. Today, I disguised as a "Cool Dude" a "Young Rebel" and in doing so, wore torn jeans, t-shirt, earrings and then shaved off my head. But then I remembered, I still had to check out of this rented place and the receptionist had seen me in my natural look and a sudden change in the look could be suspicious. I thought hard about how I could get away without inviting questions. Then I came up with a plan. I called the reception and asked for the bill. Once I knew the bill amount, I carried the bill money in my hand, packed the bag, hid the money in it, wore a hat, brown sunglasses, and ran downstairs. And on the go, dropped the keys to the receptionist alongwith with the bill money and ran out screaming, "I'm late for my fight".

After the hotel was out of sight and out of mind, I stopped at a nearby store and bought a camera. Then caught a cab to the church. Once reached, I stood outside the church to check if there was anything unusual going on. After waiting and checking for fifteen minutes, I stepped in. It was the wedding morning; people were gradually filling up the Church. There were lots of cars pulling in and around the church and walking inside wasn't easy either. One thing though, the staff at the church had done an amazing job. From funeral to a wedding, the place was flawlessly decorated.

Before going in search of the bride and the groom I wanted to see Mr. Gonzalo's cottage for one last time. Gently and steadily, hiding through the crowd, I walked to the cottage. There was nobody around and nor was there any barricade from entering the cottage. I stood there in front of it and peeked inside. The broken ceiling was back in its place. This meant that somebody knew about it, and I realized that any suspicious movement could put me in danger. I sprinted out of there at a breakneck speed.

My confidence was my disguise. I had the perfect disguise on and went straight in search of the bride and the groom. But couldn't find them as there were so many rooms and I had no time to peek in each one of them. Wedding was about to start. After wasting time and energy I was back to square one. Then in sometime the parish priest walked in and stood at the altar. It was time to start the wedding and I had no option but to get back and witness the collapse of a marriage before it started. I was feeling sorry for stealing their rings and even more sorry that I couldn't give it back before the wedding. But as I looked around, strangely everything was normal. There was no tension in the air. The "missing rings" didn't create any panic in the room.

The groom then walked in with his best man. For some god damn reason, he was wearing a pink suite and looked like a walking strawberry ice-cream. He walked straight to the alter and waited for the bride. Then the bride walked in. She was in her white gown and was looking absolutely breath-taking. Then the priest said something. I couldn't hear as I was at the back. Then the bride and groom exchanged vows which again wasn't audible and then was the time for the rings. This was the moment I was waiting for. At this moment even if I tried there was no way to help the couple. The expression on the faces of the bride and the groom would haunt me for the rest of my life if the rings weren't there and this ceremony stopped.

The best man and the bridesmaid then took a step forward and handed rings to the bride and the groom. I was relaxed and breathed a sigh of relief. I was pleased that there was no stoppage, and the wedding went as planned. I then doubted if these rings ever belonged to these couples. But you see the goodness in my heart compelled me to come back to this church to return the rings I thought belonged to the couples. I came to this wedding for no reason at all but was satisfied to see the ceremony was a success.

The bride and groom became Husband and Wife. I walked up to them and congratulated them. The couple looked at me with confusion and why not, none of them knew me and even my dress code wasn't the best fit for this wedding. People were ogling at me but that didn't bother me. I was busy clicking photos with the married couple, their parents, the church staff, and the priest. Even though I was a stranger at this wedding, I enjoyed it like it was one of his friends. This was in long time that I was happy. Then on my way out of the church I took photos of the cottage where Mr Gonzalo stayed and visited the graveyard where I stood by Mr Gonzalos tombstone to say goodbye. It was only because of Mr Gonzalo I succeeded at my first big step to becoming a successful man. I owed it to him. I had captured every part of this church, and this was a memory I intended to keep alive for the rest of my life. I knew there was something illegal going on in that church but now that I had the money, I didn't care. I walked away with more than one lakh rupees and then started the built up.

Then I robbed many more churches and targeted the black money hidden in them. Successful conversion of the first few jobs boosted my confidence and these activities increased. Once I found what I was looking for I executed the same act of stealing to perfection. Many churches changed the way of collecting and storing their white and black money and increased patrolling around the churches to catch me. The money collection bag and basket weren't carried around the church anymore. It was placed in front of the alter where the people walked up to and dropped money in it and then were carried in by the security guards. But those safeties measures couldn't stop me. I still managed to steal; this time disguised as a security guard. Eventually this news spread across all the corners of Goa, and it scared the parishes. But the sermons kept on going. I knew churches needed money to operate and as long there were God fearing people, I could always try my luck. Godless was all over the news and my frequency of stealing increased week by week. But it wasn't at all a smooth sailing.

Few were extremely close calls. On Numerous occasions I escaped by the skin of my teeth. I was becoming the Butch Cassidy of Goa and that's when people made me famous by the name, "Godless".

This was till the time I was Godless, and you know how it went. Now comes the part where the reign of Godless ended and I got involved in drug trafficking.

My success made me arrogant. When I wasn't working, I spoiled myself by drinking and gambling, I become a self-pitying booze hound. My new lifestyle increased my contacts with the people from the bad side of the society. This is what got me into the drug trafficking which was booming in Goa.

Goa had become the Las Vegas of India. From drinks to drugs to gambling everything was legal here and this attracted lots of riches and hence the demand for drugs was on the rise. Initially I was doing both stealing from churches and using that money to open channels for drugs smuggling. I bribed many cops and kept them in my pockets. It was sort of a payback for that night. I paid them for helping me expand my market coverage and I controlled many people who were garrisoned in different parts of Goa.

I earned even more money from drugs trafficking and, in few weeks, stealing from churches stopped. With drugs I came in contact with many more people from the underworld sharing same business. Some liked me and some attempted to kill me. In this rapid climb to the top of drug traffickers, I crushed many people and made more enemies than friends. I also hired many hitmen who took care of things for me. Slowly and steadily, I had built an army.

I achieved all of this, and I wasn't even thirty. When I turned twenty-eight, I was a rich man with money for a lifetime. I had achieved what I had set out to do and that too in a short span of four years. My self-confidence backed me up and anything that I touched turned to gold. But with time my mind started changing. I knew I couldn't do this for life and had to look for other legal options.

With money I bought many people in the police and government departments, in real estate, in hospitality industry with whom I started my "Legal" business. I was changing my line of work and was now a partner with one of the biggest Hotel chains in Goa. It helped me convert my black money into white. I kept the local mafia close and the cops closer. Precisely what a rich man does. I was even stepping out of the drug smuggling which I stopped completely in a year and since then I've been a generous businessman, and a close friend to everyone around me.

"So that's it, every little detail of my previous life. Now you know everything. My real name is Johnny Matthews, I changed my name to Austin Reynolds to get out of the drug business," said Austin.

It was now three in the morning and both of them still awake. Sara was so into the story that she pictured herself in Austin's story.

"Whoa! that is one heck of a story. It sounds too good to be true, just like the ones I read in the novels. I got to admit though, you are brave. How did you manage to get through this without any support" asked Sara?

"Initially I didn't need support as nobody knew who I was but then I was supported by many people who were my colleagues and some who working for me. I gotta tell you, Inspite of all the stealing from churches, I had to be God's favourite, else why would he protect me and bless me with so much of money and happiness" replied Austin.

"Maybe you are right, time will tell. One thing though, you have a Fickle mind you know that. I hope you don't get over me and find someone else" said Sara with a sarcastic smile.

"Forget moving on, I cannot even imagine my life without you. And this secret, its only you in the whole world who knows it, you can always use it to blackmail me" replied Austin with a smile.

"Your story has given me goosebumps and if I ever write a book, its going to be on your story and you will be the hero of it" said Sara and added, "what do I call you, Johnny or Austin".

"Austin, I will always be Austin for everyone now" said Austin while he laid on the bed.

"What about you brother? asked Sara, "let's talk about him tomorrow, please" replied Austin.

"Okay but is there anything that you are not telling me. Now is the time to speak up," said Sara.

Austin had many more secrets to reveal. Though he was out of the drugs business he continued paying off the local officials and the politicians. He knew crossing lines with them wasn't a good idea. The lion had to lie down with the lamb. But because he paid off so many people his life was important to them. They did everything to protect him, they knew killing him would be like killing the goose who laid golden egg. He purposely kept this part away from Sara not because he forgot but Austin didn't want Sara to be concerned or to worry about any kind of danger that may befall on them. So, now he was into two minds and said to himself, 'why not' there wouldn't be a time better than this.

He got up, walked away from Sara, picked up a glass of water, took a sip and said, "You better sit down. There are many more things to come. But you should know that I am not going to ask you to promise me anything. I am leaving our future in your hands". This words from Austin scared Sara.

"What is it now, you are scaring me" she asked.

"I wasn't a drug lord, per se, I helped the dealers in moving drugs in different parts of Goa and the surroundings. And in doing so, I paid many cops and officials and sometime had to take drastic methods like threatening or kidnapping. But I never put a finger on anyone... I hired people to do it".

Sara responded sarcastically, "That's good to know that you didn't hit people yourself and paid others to do it, something that you denied few seconds ago. But go on what else".

"Nothing more. One day I got up and decided I didn't want to be a part of it anymore and left" said Austin and he sat down feeling relieved that he had told all his dark secrets to Sara and there was nothing else to worry.

Then Sara replied, "ok. Let's recap. You have been involved in multiple robberies, drug trafficking, bribing the cops, kidnapping, and threatening people. These are lot of crimes. Is there anything illegal left to do?".

"Umm. I guess no" nodded Austin and said "Whatever you decide, I will go with it. If you want to call the cops you can. I have done the crime and I am not afraid to do the time,".

Sara had a decision to make. Whether to call the cops or to forget about the past and continue seeing Austin. After all she was now part of it. In the eyes of law, Sara was a party to crime and could be charged and convicted in court if all these secrets ever came out. This was a life changing decision for her.

"It's late and I need time to process. Will talk about it tomorrow".

Sara switched off the lights and went to sleep. Austin laid on the bed too. Both of them laid at opposite sides of the beds but both were awake.

In few minutes the lights came back on. Sara turned around and it was Austin who had switched them on.

"I am so sorry I missed out one part. I think it's important you know".

Sara didn't get up, "tell me I am listening".

"Umm, you know Kalyan right" asked Austin.

"Our Chef? what about him" she asked.

"Nothing, just that he worked with me during my drug trafficking days and umm... he is a Hitman".

Austin immediately turned off the lights and laid on the bed while Sara sat there like a statue. Sara then got up, carried her pillow and bedsheet to other room. Both of them spend nights in different rooms but none of them slept.

Next morning as the sun came out, Austin laid on his bed looking outside the window when Sara walked in. "Good morning" greeted Austin.

"Shut up and listen" replied Sara and added, "Whatever you told me last night was too much and I am willing to let it all go if you promise me that you would never step back into that world again".

"I promise and sorry to put you through all of this. One more thing. Nobody here knows anything about it. Even Kalyan doesn't know that I was Godless. Let's keep it that way" Sara agreed and replied, "Don't worry. I would take it to my grave. Now tell me about Kalyan" she asked.

Sara had mentioned that she was into books and criminal stories which is why she fell in love with "Godless". But Sara's interest in hearing about Kalyan's story made him realize that Sara was not only in into the books filled with crimes and underworld she was possessed with it. He thought this could be a condition and maybe she needed to see a psychiatrist.

But maybe later, now it was the time to tell her about Kalyan.

"Ok, the story telling continues" replied Austin sarcastically and added, "On my way to the top I had many enemies and was constantly at war with them. In that battlefield I made a friend, Kalyan. He joined as an apprentice and slowly became a good and a loyal friend. Kalyan was a smart chap, and this erudite guy had a master's degree. His suggestions were often accepted by me and my colleagues. It was Kalyan who suggested me to change my identity and move out of Goa if I ever planned on getting myself out of drug trafficking. But I was in love with Goa and hence I agreed for a new identity but insisted I stay. Kalyan became my right hand and took care of things for me that too without getting noticed. He was swift and that's why he was deadly. Nobody knew it was Kalyan who was cleaning up my enemies and together we were indomitable. With contacts, I made sure everything about my past was erased from the government databases leaving no trace. Once everything was clean, Johnny died, and Austin Reynolds was born. I changed my name to leave my past behind so that nobody came back to bite me in my new future. But there were few officials and partners who had seen my face and Kalyan made sure they were taken care of. I had seen in the movies how the life ended for drug traffickers, and so I considered Kalyan's suggestion to come clean. I was a business minded guy and wanted to expand my legacy. Slowly, I took over many businesses in different domains and became one of the richest men In Goa. Again, Kalyan helped me all the way and then with a new name, came a brand-new businessman. He's an evil genius."

Austin took a sigh of relief. "let's not talk about any of this now. Please let go of it" Austin said to Sara.

"This is surprising. How can a sweet man like Kalyan be a killer? I like the food he cooks. I am still not able see him as a Hitman" replied Sara with a surprise and added, "should I be scared of him".

"Just like me, he was also a victim of the society and the situation. But he is loyal to me, and you don't have to be scared. He is a saint, and he loves me. I respect him and he is my closest friend. He would have been at a higher post in any of my business, but he isn't interested in money. He likes to cook and hence chose to stay with me as my chef".

This calmed Sara but she wasn't finished, "Your brother, where is he now. Let's go get him back".

Austin stood up, "whoa it's not that easy. I haven't spoken to him for years and don't even know if he is in Mumbai or someplace else. There is no way I can find him" replied Austin.

"Why did he change his name too" Sara asked sarcastically and "no" nodded Austin. Then to stay away from this discussion, he got down from the bed and sprinted into the bathroom.

Sara left the room, but she didn't let this discussion go by. She didn't have a family, but it meant a lot to her. She played a pivotal role in bringing them together. Sara spoke to Austin about visiting his brother constantly for days and finally Austin gave up and agreed to it. When Austin agreed to make amends with his brother, Sara was delighted but Austin wasn't. He still held a grudge of how things were in the past.

Austin didn't have the contact information of his brother or any of his friends from Mumbai. But he remembered where his brother last stayed. So now it would be a surprise drop in rather than a planned and informed visit to Franky's place whom he had not seen or spoken to for years. Austin wasn't even sure if Franky would even accept him but for the sake of Sara, he went with it. It was planned on the coming Saturday morning.

It was Saturday and time for a reality check. Franklin has the day off on Saturdays but this morning he was at the house at eight. An hour before Austin and Sara were to leave for Mumbai. He wanted to be a part of this visit.

"It's Saturday. What the hell are you doing here" asked Austin while walking down the stairs for breakfast.

"You once said to me that I am your brother from another mother. Now that you have a real one, I want to see him in person. Please don't deny" replied Franklin.

"How did you know? asked Austin.

"Sara told me. She asked for my help in trying to convince you to visit your brother. But I wanted that decision be entirely yours." replied Franklin.

"What else did she tell you" Austin got scared thinking Sara might have told him few things more which wasn't to be disclosed. But it turned out there was nothing else to worry. Austin also knew Kalyan had told Franklin few of his secrets and he intended to find it out soon.

Once they finished their breakfast, they were on their way. Austin and Franklin were in suits while Sara surprisingly wore a saree. It was an eight hour-long journey from Goa and midway Chris slept. He didn't get up till they reached the destination. Everyone in the car slept apart from Austin and the driver. Austin was excited but also scared. 'What if Franky rejected and insulted them all. He wouldn't be able to live with the insult of his close ones and there was no proof either that Franky was alive, What if he's dead'. Negative thoughts like these kept him up. Austin had abandoned his brother for years and wasn't even sure if Franky still stayed at the place where they were visiting.

When they reached Mumbai, Austin was surprised to see lot of changes around since he last stepped foot here years ago. There were many tall buildings around and finding the correct way to the house was like finding a needle in a stack of hay. Good thing was that their old playground was still there, and his house was near to it. While circling around the ground, watching the kids play, brought back many childhood memories of him and his friends spending almost an entire day out on the ground playing cricket or football. Suddenly Austin wasn't scared anymore. In fact, he was eager to meet his brother and friends and in some time they reached. The road wasn't big enough for the car to drive in, so they all got down and walked while the driver parked the car to other side of the ground. Chris was still sleeping on Austin's shoulder. While they gently walked to the house, he could recognize few of the shops in the area, but the shopkeepers didn't recognize him. These shops were now run by their children.

After walking for five minutes, they reached the building. It was a two-storey building and looked hundred years old. Austin stayed on the first floor and so they walked upstairs and there it was. Austin saw the brown coloured door of his house and instantly froze. They all stopped couple of steps from the door. Austin couldn't move but Sara encouraged him. When they neared the door the name tag on the door wasn't his brother's. So, he rang the doorbell and what Austin feared…happened.

There was someone else staying in that house and on enquiring about Franky the residents had no clue about it. They bought this house from someone who had purchased it from Franky.

This was what Austin feared and expected to happen. This long journey was a huge waste of time. Austin also spoke to the neighbours on the floor, but nobody knew about Franky or his whereabouts. Disappointed, they all walked downstairs. There was nothing else left to do but to go back home. Chris was now up and was hungry. They decided to get something to eat and then proceed their journey back to Goa. They sat in the car and drove but soon stopped at a nearby restaurant for snacks.

"At least we tried" said Sara and cheered Austin. Once they finished their snacks they sat in the car and were on their way back.

Suddenly a couple guys on bike stopped in front of the car. This scared Austin. This is exactly what had happened few months ago and he feared this was again an attack on him. But luckily it wasn't. These guys were Austin's childhood friends and had got the news of Austin's arrival. These guys approached the vehicle and Austin recognized them. It was Abdul and Sandy. He got down from the car and hugged them.

"It's so good to see you, how have you been?" asked Austin.

"Things are good. Life is good" said Abdul and added, "c'mon, let's go to the ground and talk. We are blocking the traffic".

Then they all went back to the ground. Austin on Abdul's bike and Franklin, Sara, and Chris in the car. Once they reached the ground the driver parked the car. Sara and Chris stayed inside while Abdul, Sandy, Austin, and Franklin talked about Franky.

Abdul started by telling Austin everything that happened since the day he left.

"After you abandoned us all, you brother went to the cops in the hope that they might find you and bring you back. Days turned to weeks and weeks to months. The cops couldn't trace you. But Franky never gave up. He did every damn thing possible from bribing the cops to threatening them, but nothing worked. With mom and you both gone from his life, Franky was weakened but he respected his life and so he got back to his feet, got himself a decent job and worked on "staying alive". He never stopped visiting the cops, never lost hope. It was terrible time for him where even his marriage fell apart and his wife left him for someone else. After couple of years, he got posted to another place and had to move out. He is married the second time and has a kid".

Austin had tears in his eyes "he's married again and has a kid?".

"Yes, and that's all I know about your brother. He never came back and sold this house few months later. It's so good to see you. Where have you been all this time" asked Abdul.

"I went to Goa and luckily did well" replied Austin.

"Yeah, we can see that" Abdul responded sarcastically pointing to the Jaguar that they drove in.

"Do you know how can I find him? Can anyone help me with his address?" asked Austin.

"Yes, I will text you, his address. Share me your contact number" replied Sandy.

Once Austin got the address, he couldn't wait but to go to see his brother. With a promise to stay in touch with Abdul and Sandy he got back to the car. Before entering the car Franklin, asked, "who is Johnny? why were they calling you Johnny?".

"Not the place, nor the time" replied Austin and got in the car. Austin then realized maybe Kalyan didn't tell Franklin everything. On the other hand, Sara knew everything but acted surprised in front of Franklin.

This time Austin took the front seat punched the address into the GPS and they drove away. From Andheri to Vashi, as per the GPS, it was two hours' drive.

The address he was texted had the building and the flat number and they reached there at six in the evening. It was a huge society with at least eight buildings in total and as they drove in, in a Jaguar, they weren't even stopped by the guard. They got down at the mentioned apartment and walked toward the lift. This was a twenty-storey apartment and Franky stayed on tenth. While waiting for the lift Austin went through the name tags of all the owners on the board and was delighted to see his brother's name. Unlike Austin, he went on with the same name.

When they reached the floor and as soon as the lift door opened, Austin rushed towards the room number 1008. Rang the bell and the door was opened by the maid.

"Franky's house?" asked Austin and the maid nodded yes.

"Who is it" Franky asked from inside.

'Koi aapko milne aaya hain saab" said the maid and she went back inside. Then came Franky at the door. At first, he didn't recognize Austin but then, "Johnny is it you" he asked "yes" replied Austin and they hugged.

Both of them were in tears. Then Franky invited them inside and while stepping inside, Sara looked at Franklin, "Johnny? who the hell is that" and Franklin replied, "Not the place, nor the time".

Franky called his wife and his son and introduced Austin to them. Austin introduced Sara, Franklin, and Chris. Franky had a six-year-old son named Jonathan who invited Chris to join him for video games in the next room. At first Chris hesitated but then he went along.

Strangely nor Franky nor Austin spoke anything about their past and their whereabouts. Both of them were happy to see each other and didn't want their bitter history to ruin the moment. They spoke about their business and Austin told everything about his hotels while Franky was a successful investment banker.

With so much to talk they all lost track of time and it was dinner time. Austin and team hadn't planned on waiting till dinner as they had a long journey back, but Franky insisted them to stay the night. Austin then called the driver for dinner.

Franky's house was a huge four room apartment with a separate room for servants where the driver slept the night. Franky asked Austin to occupy the guest room which was big enough for them. Franklin crashed on the couch in the hall while Franky, his wife and kid slept in their bedroom.

When Austin entered the guest room, he saw a wall full of photos. It was a wall full of Austin's photos.

"Did you think I would forget my little brother" said Franky and left the room while Austin stood there admiring the wall. Chris was tired and immediately dozed off. Austin went through each photo and remembered the time which he spoke about to Sara. In sometime Sara slept too but Austin couldn't. Then after twisting and turning sides on the bed for some time, he stepped out of the room and walked into the gallery. He sat alone for some time and was then joined by Franky with drinks in his hands.

"Even you couldn't sleep huh!" asked Franky, "lot of things on my mind" replied Austin.

Franky wanted to deep dive into Austin's life and so he gently swopped in the topic.

"Remember when we were kids. How we played video games together. Today seeing Chris and Jonathan brought back those memories" "yeah, we played 'Mario brother' and 'Contra' and I always kicked your ass" replied Austin with smile on their faces. "TO OLD TIMES" they both cheersed their whiskey glasses and just then Franky swooped in.

"What happened Johnny. Why did you abandon me without any reason? You don't know what hell I've been through since then. Not a day goes by without remembering you. I expected you to be by my side. We could have talked about things that were troubling you. We could have worked It out," said Franky.

"Talk? after so many years do you seriously want to go down that road. You want to talk about it, then let's talk. I came to you many times, but you never had time for me or for my problems. You had time only for your precious wife who eventually left you. You couldn't wait. You had to marry even before mom's ashes cooled down. How selfish could you be and don't think I didn't know about you telling on my friends which drove them away. You took my life from me, and I had to start a new one. Don't you dare blame it on me"? Franky was stunned that Austin blamed him for everything, but he became the bigger man and accepted it.

"You blame me, I'm fine with that. But remember she was my mother too. She was close to me the same way she was to you and her passing by was something that I couldn't make peace with initially. But you are right. I am the elder brother and should have taken care of you in that difficult time. I am sorry for everything. Let's bury the hatchet and make this a new beginning" Both agreed to it and then Franky asked Johnny about the time he disappeared and it whereabouts.

That's when Austin took out his cell phone, "Type my name". Franky typed in Johnny Mathews, his original name but nothing came up.

"What am I looking at" asked confused Franky. "Sorry my mistake, type in Austin Reynolds" and Franky was surprised to see the details unloaded on the page. The search displayed the number of businesses Austin owned.

"Who is Austin and why is he looking exactly like you" asked the still confused Franky.

"Not like me, it is me. I changed my name to start a new life. This was what I do now." Replied Austin.

"This says you own multiple chain of hotel across states' read Franky

"Yep, that's right" "wow you are a rich guy now. Owning hotels in Goa. Hey, I hope I get the family & friends discount if I ever plan to stay at one of your hotels" Franky asked with a huge mirth and Austin replied, "You let me know when you plan to come. The entire hotel and the staff would be at your service. You have my word". "Thanks bro, but tell me one thing, what do I call you 'Johnny' or 'Austin'" These were the exact words that Sara had used few days ago and Austin replied, "Johnny, I will always be Johnny to you".

Franky never asked Austin how he got there or how he became such a successful person. He knew it wasn't something that they both were comfortable talking about right now. "TO LIFE" they both cheersed their last drink and called it a night.

Next morning after breakfast Austin and team left for Goa and assured to stay in touch. Austin realized Franky never asked about Sara and Chris which was strange. But it didn't bother him. He still felt the rush. It happened. He was back on speaking terms with his brother. This was the best thing that happened to Austin, and it was possible only because of Sara for which Austin thanked Sara and was forever grateful to her.

This was an emotional and eventful weekend and Franklin continued to note it in his diary. He didn't perform any stand up for months but had never given up taking notes. He now had so much content in that diary that he could easily be a Comedian or an Author.

On their way back Austin realized he had everything that a man can ever want in his life. He had money, had his family, and promised himself to take care of them till his last breath. Only thing that bothered him was his attacker. He was still out there which was a dangerous thing.

On the other hand, Franklin was with Austin for more than a year now and witnessed everything that changed around. He was glad this was transpiring but one thing bothered him. As per Kalyan, earlier in Austin's life, on the road to success Austin joined hands with many people in the dark side of the society. Few were taken care of and few powerful were untouchable even to Austin. Now on the road of being a glorified soul he was upsetting same people by breaching agreements and denying their unlawful deals. Austin had become a thorn in their flesh and that scared Franklin.

Sara was the best thing Austin could have ever asked for. She brought back Austin's brother, united Chris with his grandfather, gave Chris his childhood, gave shelter to an old man and many more such act of random kindness. They also opened a school which took in the orphans, gave them a place to stay and took care of their hunger. Then they expanded and built a church and taught the kids about God and Christianity. Like every other church, conducted frequent sermons for the people. Inauguration of this church was a special one. Austin and Sara got married that day and the rings were the same one which Austin had stolen from the church where he met Mr Gonzalo. He had a special connection to it. Sara was aware of it but as these rings had a sentimental value to Austin, she agreed to use these rings. Finally, they tied the knot. Finally, the family was complete.

That day Sara had tears in her eyes. She never imagined her life would turn out to be this great. Sara was relieved that she didn't handover Austin to the cops that night and went with her heart. This indeed was the right decision, and she was thankful to God for everything.

With all the good things happening in life Austin got closer to God. After all God gave him a family. He made peace with God and asked him for forgiveness for robbing his houses. Unfortunately for Austin just when he kneeled before God and asked for forgiveness, things changed.

After few months, Sara's old gang 'The Saviours' invited her to join on a bike trip to Jaisalmer, Rajasthan, to explore the royal palaces. One of their crew members was getting married in Jaisalmer and the whole gang opted to make it a bike trip. It was a long-needed break for everyone and a time to catch up after a long time. Sara hadn't spent time with her friends since she met Austin and desperately missed the excitement and the thrill of riding bike with them.

But time had changed. She had responsibilities and going on this trip was now becoming a distant dream.

Sara didn't mention anything about it to Austin for the few days and hadn't declined the invitation either. Her heart wanted to go but every other part of the body denied. This was eating her inside. The concern here was not that she couldn't go if she wanted to. The problem was leaving everyone alone for fifteen days.

Finally, she told Austin about the trip. At first Austin wasn't willing to let her go on this long trip alone but he saw the eagerness in her eyes and recommended that he accompanied her on this adventure. This way she wouldn't be alone, and they could take turns driving. Austin was scared but didn't display it. This idea delighted Sara but what about Chris? since they all got back together this was the first time Chris wouldn't be part of a trip. After giving it a lot of thought Austin and Sara discussed this with Franklin and grandfather. It was agreed to leave Chris with his grandfather and Franklin. The only people he trusted.

Austin was also planning a trip just for two of them since long and this invitation came at the right time. It was an extremely long journey of about three thousand kilometres to and fro stretching this trip for over fifteen days.

A guy roaming around in extravagance car had to get used to sitting on a bike for longs hours and so Austin practiced it daily for the next fifteen days. This trip was a fortnight away now and daily morning Austin and Sara rode the bike. Primarily for one hour and then extended it for two hours.

Austin had learned to ride a bike and practicing it daily improved his confidence and balance especially with Sara on the back seat. Initial plan was that they both rode individual bikes but then realizing how tiring it could be they decided to go with one bike and take turns driving it. They even bought a new bike specially for this trip. It was a superfast two hundred cc bullet.

As the day of the trip neared shopping for it was almost done. Sara was excited but out of the two Austin was most thrilled. He was eagerly waiting for them to embark on this long-awaited adventure.

Before going on the trip Austin had to manage his businesses in such a way that he wasn't bothered and there was no impact on the business whatsoever. Austin trusted nobody but Franklin and so he drafted a power of attorney in the name of Franklin and got busy planning itineraries for the trip.

On one hand Franklin felt burdened with the load but on the other hand this "Load" was his biggest opportunity to learn how to handle businesses. He understood that such experience can be gained only by handling actual transactions. He was practically owning the empire of Austin and felt the power Austin possessed.

It was a long drive from Goa to Jaisalmer and they had to break journey to be able to drive all the way. Austin wasn't a biker since beginning but Sara was. So, it was Sara who jotted the itinerary for the entire trip which involved stays and site seeing at famous location. The plan was to start from Goa and major halt was at Pune which was around eight hours and five hundred kilometres from Goa. Then the halt was scheduled at Mumbai, Vadodara, Gir sasan where they would enjoy the safari, then halt at Pali to check out the famous Bangar museum and finally the last stop, 'Jaisalmer'. So far, the itinerary looked good and now they only had to count the days.

As the rest of the gang was from multiple regions in and outside of Maharashtra, they planned to meetup at Vadodara, in Gujrat. Austin and Sara were alone for nine hundred kilometres which they decided to cover over the next three days with halts at multiple locations.

Finally, the day had come. The bullet kick started in the morning at four and the sound of bullet echoed in the quiet morning like machine gun firing. It was really cold, and Sara took the first turn to drive. With matching jackets and helmets they looked professional bikers and doomed to catch attention of the passer-by.

After two hours of drive first break was at the top of a valley, named 'Amboli Ghat' famous for its waterfall. This waterfall is the "place to see" during the monsoon. But this was November. Even though there was no water in the 'waterfall', this spot had an added beauty of the astonishing view of the green valley spread across acres of land covered with white clouds and the adjoining mountains. Sara did an excellent job driving all the way till here in extremely low visibility.

The first light of the sun piercing through the trees made it a view never to forget. Sara and Austin reached there at six thirty in the morning and they just sat there on the ledge and took in the nature. There was pin drop silence with no vehicles passing by. Cup of tea and Maggie was an energy booster which they needed for another few hours of drive. After relaxing for thirty minutes, they were on the way. As the day passed the traffic on the roads and the heat increased and the drive became hectic. This was just the first three hundred kilometres, and they were having thoughts of turning back especially Austin, who had never been on such a long bike trip in his entire life. Although he enjoyed it, the first three hundred kilometres was playing games with his minds. Sara on the other hand was still excited. Sara's earlier bike trips were with twenty other bikers which gave her the feeling of a 'Queen marching her army' and this was her first solo trip with her husband which gave her the feeling of 'Being a wife' carrying her husband on her bike. Not to mention how uncomfortable they were due to the sweating generated by the leather jackets.

Their second stop was at Kolhapur where they halted for breakfast. There was silence between them, and Austin felt the exhilaration gradually turning into frustration. Suddenly, he had an idea. It wasn't a good one but as long as he had one, he put it out on the table. The idea was to skip the drive on the bike and spare the pain and frustration. In place of Rajasthan, the idea was to visit his farmhouse in Panvel, spend couple of days there and then catch a flight to Jaipur.

Austin wasn't sure if Sara would agree to it but when she heard it, she was all into it. The look on Sara's faced changed completely. She wasn't the wild and rebel kind like she was earlier, she had changed and so she agreed to this plan. Now that both agreed to the change in the destination, they had to think of an excuse to tell their biker friends, to Franklin and Chris.

Excitement filled them with adrenaline, and they just wanted to reach the farmhouse as early as possible and then maybe come up with some lame excuses that sounded true.

This secret place in Panvel was kind of a den for Austin in case he had to hide from his enemies. Austin had built many getaway houses across multiple locations of Maharashtra and this one at Panvel was the closest one. Austin had been here couple of times in the initial days with few colleagues, but it was first time with Sara. In fact, Sara wasn't even aware this place existed. Austin too had forgotten about this place and remembered it today. So, when Austin told her about it, Sara was full of questions. She turned from being a friend to being a wife, questioning all the details while Austin was being a lame husband and apologizing constantly.

They reached this place somewhere in the evening at around six. On the way they picked few things to eat. No problem with the drinks. It was always loaded in all of Austin's houses and was available at one's convenience. There was a huge bar inside the house.

This place was massive and was being taken care by an old man and his wife since years. They stayed there in the servant quarters and were house sitting. When the house was empty it was practically theirs and they lived here like they owned it. Austin knew that but as long as the house was taken care of, he didn't bother.

He had given them freedom and access to each and every room in the house except one. This one on the top floor was locked and the access codes to it were only with Austin. Nobody knew what was behind the doors and Austin made sure nobody even came close to finding it.

Once freshened up, Austin and Sara got back to planning their routine for the next few days and the enthusiasm was out of the roof, they were so excited.

Sara's friends were supposed to meet them halfway the next morning which wasn't going to happen now. Sara called them and told them, that as some urgent business had to be taken care of and they would meet them directly at the destination. This was a lie and some of the friends had suspected it, but they went with it. Friends were taken care off and now it was time to tell Franklin. Not that it was needed but still it was a good thing that Franklin knew their whereabouts. Austin told Franklin about this sudden change of plans but didn't disclose anything about the house.

Now that the "updating people" part was done, it was time to get back to the reality. It was eight in the evening, and both were sipping drinks and munching snacks while watching movies. They had nothing to do, and the movie marathon was on.

Sara was a fan of action movies while Austin's genre had changed from adventure to romance since he met Sara. They couldn't settle on a movie with both action and romance in it. So, they decided to select the genre alphabetically. It was time for 'Action'.

Sara was a biker and she embraced speed and adventure. The first movie that played wasn't a surprise. It was "Fast and Furious". Austin downloaded both the parts and started off with the first one.

As the movie progressed the intake of drinks increased and eventually the "Drunken Drama" started. One of them was highly intoxicated and it wasn't Austin. Sara had lost her senses after an entire bottle of whiskey and first two parts of "Fast and Furious". Now she was displaying Austin how 'fast' she was by running around the house while the 'furious' Austin chased her. This childish behaviour of Sara annoyed Austin but he was the only one who had to handle her, and he did. In some time, she was knocked out and Austin carried her to the bedroom to put her to sleep. Once she was in deep sleep Austin walked upstairs to his secret room.

A movie fanatic rich man with many secrets and this one was just like the ones in spy movies. An uncrackable metal door with codes divided his two worlds. This room was filled with antiques and there were many famous paintings, sculptures, and guess what…loads of cash lying around. That's not all there was something else too hidden behind a huge bookstack. Austin pushed a hidden button on one of the statues in the room and the book stack opened. It made way to a wall which pulled out automatically. On that wall were guns, lots, and lots of guns. Even though Austin didn't use guns he was a huge collector of them. These guns were worth millions in the black-market, but he never sold any of them. Same way these paintings and sculptures were expensive which

Austin never even thought of selling. Maybe he feared it would trace back to him. He trusted nobody and knew someday someone would surely stab him in the back. Nobody knew if Austin stole them or bought them. Nobody knew this room existed. This was a secret from everyone and even his 'partner in crime' Kalyan wasn't aware of it. Then, post checking his treasured collection, Austin walked out and went back to the bed.

Next morning, they both took a walk in the woods. Holding each other's hands, they walked for about thirty minutes and then turned back towards the house. On their way back Sara felt like somebody was shadowing them. This place in the woods was creepy one like the ones they show in horror movies and they both being a movieholic, were scared. Her grip on Austin's hands tightened and that's when Austin realized that Sara was scared. He stopped, put his arm around Sara, pulled her close and asked, "Are you alright'. Sara nodded yes. Austin wasn't convinced, he asked her again, "are you scared"? shivering Sara replied, "No", "then please let go the tight grip, my palm is about to break" said Austin and the grip was loosened.

Austin knew Sara was scared, so he decided to have some fun. He started telling Sara a story about one mystical incident involving a family that stayed in his house before he bought it. Sara replied, "yeah I would like to know how you got yourself this gorgeous house."

Austin had bought this barren land and built this house on it. It was a business deal. But he made up this story for Sara just to creep her out.

"You know I ran away leaving my family and friends behind and came to Goa, well before Goa, I stopped at one place near the city right here in Panvel and took a job at a small roadside restaurant. This was something I had to do to avoid dying of hunger and I needed money. That's where I learned how a restaurant functioned.

My boss Mr. Govind Verma was super rich guy and had many businesses outside this restaurant. His restaurant business was just a cover up to hide all the illegal activities that he was involved in. He was famous for all the wrong reasons and that is what came back to bite him. While climbing the ladder to success he ruined many lives. One-night these same people invaded this house and killed him, his wife and their ten years old daughter in the same bedroom that we sleep in".

This story was fake, but the way Austin went on describing it gave Sara chills and as Austin expected, she believed every word he said. Again, she got lost into the story and there was an immediate effect to this. Sara was scared to go back into the house. Then Austin cooled her off and told her that this was a story from one of the movies he had seen few years ago and there was nothing to worry. Sara getting lost into such stories was something that worried Austin and he decided to talk to an expert about it once they got back.

They both then walked inside and continued planning their trip. They booked air tickets to Jodhpur as Jaisalmer is not directly connected by air and couriered their bike as they had to show they drove all the way. From Jodhpur, it was around three hundred kilometres to Jaisalmer and Sara and Austin agreed to cover this distance on their bike.

Flight was scheduled to reach jodhpur two days prior to the ceremony and the guests were hosted at a hotel few minutes of drive from the wedding hall.

Sara and Austin reached jodhpur right on time and after waiting for couple of hours at the airport lounge, they got their bike delivered to the main gate of the airport. Then…the adventure began.

They even changed their attire and transformed from looking 'Royals' wearing suites to 'Rebel' in jeans and jackets.

As they had to drive a long way, they didn't carry much of luggage and decided to buy from the local stores. The only thing they carried in that backpack was their dresses that they were to wear during the wedding. Sara was planning to wear an ethnic Saree and Austin a traditional Sherwani. When they reached, carrying these dressed turned out to be a good idea as there was no shops nearby. They had just avoided a dressing disaster.

They reached the destination after driving for four. Sara's friends were already there and gave Sara and Austin one heck of a welcome. Sara was no more the leader of their gang but was still treated with dignity and respect and to display their affection, Sara and Austin were allotted a separate room which was even decorated while the others shared a dormitory. Austin was super impressed with the welcome and the hospitality and instantly gelled with the group. After a round of introduction with all of Sara's friend's, Sara and Austin went to their room to freshen up.

When they came down the dinner was about to set and in the interim the drinks were on. Everyone having a wonderful time and in sometime the party moved up on the roof. Telling jokes and singing songs, everyone was having lot of fun. Austin was having a great time and he thanked Sara for making him a part of it. Although the start of this trip was a little shaky the end was surely going to be memorable.

As the evening enlivened Sara became the centre of discussion. Sara's friends revealed many secrets of Sara to Austin and all of them were mostly about charity. It turned out that Sara was a follower of Mother Teresa and was involved in many acts of kindness which also included nights she spent distributing food and blankets to the homeless during the chilly winter nights. There were many such acts and surprisingly Austin had no clue about them. Austin had experienced Sara's kindness since he knew her, but all of this was unimaginable. In the eyes of Austin, Sara was a saviour sent by God and maybe that's why she named her posse "The Saviours". That moment Austin was in tears, but he hid it from everyone while he held Sara in his arms. Their love for each other grew.

Austin and Sara were having a blast at the wedding, and they didn't want it to stop. But like all the good things it had to end. Austin was unhappy knowing that once the wedding was over everyone would part ways and to ensure they have such a good time again, Austin invited all of them to his holiday home in Goa. An all-expense paid trip on a special occasion. It was Sara's birthday, and it was coming up in few of weeks.

Although Austin had only two weeks to plan and arrange everything, Sara insisted Austin to extend their current stay for few more days, to explore a mysterious temple in Rajasthan known as, as "Bullet Baba's Temple". It was a biker's creed.

This was the first time Austin heard about it and immediately assumed it to be rubbish and tried to convince Sara to drop this stupid idea.

As per the local's this temple is a memorial in Pali district of Jodhpur, devoted to a divinity in the form of a bullet bike, a motorcycle. India is a mysterious land, and this story lived up to that reputation.

Sara told Austin that, "This temple is devoted to a biker who died here in Jodhpur in a fatal bike accident. Crazy thing is that when the cops took this bike to the police station it disappeared few times and was found at the place of accident. This news spread across the village like a forest fire and the people believed that the spirit of the biker moved this bike around assuming it wasn't his time to die. So, to free his spirit and for the biker to rest in peace, the people built him this temple, kept this bike in it as an Idol and worshipped it. This is not the only strange thing.

People also say that if anyone drives past this temple without offering, they never reach the destination without harming themselves. So, each and every person may he be on a bike or a car or in a bus stops at this temple to offer prayers. This place has witnessed many miracles since then".

Austin didn't believe it, but Sara wanted to explore. Austin had only one thing on his mind and that was to get back home as early as possible. He was feeling homesick and also had to make so many arrangements from ticket reservation for at least ten people, their arrangement to stay and food and beverages. Although Austin had Franklin who was excellent when it came to planning a party, but Austin wanted to do it himself as it was for Sara's birthday.

Austin tried to talk Sara out of it, but she insisted. "I know you are excited but trust me this much of effort and time in seeing this place would be a disappoint. I know it" said Austin and an argument broke out between them. Sara was so angry that she decided to visit this temple on her own but then Austin gave up and agreed to accompany her but didn't stop trash talking about this temple all the way. He went from all romantic to irritative that too in front of few of their friends. Sara had hard time understanding why Austin hated this place so much and why was he trying to get them out of visiting it.

The wedding was now over, and everyone went back home. The visit to this mysterious temple was scheduled next morning. At seven in the morning Austin and Sara got all ready to ride their bike on this last adventure of this trip. This trip was merely fifty to sixty kilometres from where they were staying. A drive of couple of hours.

There was a reason behind Austin's reluctance to visit this place and it was because of a nightmare he had few nights before. He felt like something bad was about to happen, but he didn't mention this to Sara as it sounded silly. Today's visit to this temple was a call of destiny.

Halfway to this temple they stopped for snacks at a local restaurant and even then, Austin kept on blabbering about not visiting the temple. After a halt of twenty minutes, they were on the way. In some time, they were within couple of kilometres from the temple and that's when Austin's nightmare come true. Something happened.

Austin was driving at a speed of sixty and at a hairpin like turn their bike slipped. The speed dragged both of them for few meters. Austin managed to get away with scratches and bruises but was unable to lift himself up. Austin was conscious and was helped by the people who gathered post witnessing this accident. Sara was unconscious. Her head hit the concrete road and was bleeding badly. The locals rushed for their help and immediately carried them to the nearby hospital. It was like Austin was being punished for all the bad things he said about 'Bullet baba' the entire way. It was the curse of 'Bullet baba'.

At the hospital post getting the initial treatment and few pain killers, Austin ran towards Sara who was in the Intensive care unit of the hospital, fighting for her life. Sara's condition was very critical, doctors had almost given up, but Austin hadn't.

Franklin flew in that evening and was shocked to see Sara fighting for her life. He just sat there outside the room while Austin sat beside Sara's bed the entire evening. Sara was too precious to be gone. In the hope that Sara's condition would improve Austin didn't move an inch away from her bed that night. He held her close all the time. Praying to God begging her life back. Then out of nowhere one of the hospital staff members approached Austin. This guy had a soft corner to accident cases involving 'Bullet baba temple' and so he had walked in to talk to Austin.

"Sir, I know it's not the right time, but may I speak to you for a minute" asked the hospital employee but Austin didn't even acknowledge. The guy asked again, and this time Austin agreed to talk to him. They both walked out of the ICU and to the nearby corridor.

"Sir, I know madam's condition is not good and I wish she gets well soon" said the hospital employee. This got Austin furious, "this is what you wanted to talk about? are you crazy. I appreciate your sentiment, but are you crazy?" Austin rampaged on and on… "no sir no. I came to suggest you go back to where this happened and offer your prayers. I have seen miracles happen…that place is miraculous" and the guy left. Austin didn't bother to even consider what he suggested. He thought it was nonsense and went back to Sara.

Austin had been at Sara's bed for about six hours now and the sun was out. The next morning Sara was visited by a senior doctor who was assigned to this case. Franklin who was waiting outside the ICU walked in with the doctor and shook Austin who had fallen asleep on the chair. The doctor examined Sara and they both stood there with eyes wide opened hoping for some good news. While the doctor was going through the report nothing could be predicted from his facial expression. His expression never changed.

"Please call her family and friends. Her condition has worsened. She might not come back" said the doctor and he walked out of the room signalling something to the nurse.

Austin broke in tears and collapsed on the ground. Franklin picked him up and sat him on the chair holding him in his arms, comforting him. That's when Austin remembered the little weird conversation, he had with the staff member.

"Franklin, please get the car. I want to go back to the temple" said Austin and stood up. Franklin couldn't believe that Austin wanted to go out rather than staying at the hospital. He thought Austin had lost his mind.

"Please hold yourself together, be strong" said Franklin but Austin was adamant and insisted to give him the car keys. Franklin asked the reason behind it and Austin said, "a guy came to me in the room, took me to the corridor and told me to offer prayers to the bullet baba temple. It's my only chance to save Sara".

Franklin knew this was crazy but then he realized he was sitting outside the room this whole time and never saw Austin come out or go back to the room. He asked, "when did this happen? I was sitting outside the room since last evening and never saw you coming out or any guy go in".

"Few hours ago. He was the staff of the hospital wearing a grey coloured shirt. He came in the room and talked to me".

Austin sensed Franklin didn't believe him and so went in hunt of the guy. Now the point was to prove Franklin that he wasn't making it up and was telling the truth. After searching the hospital end to end Austin didn't find him. He came back and sat next to Franklin knowing that Franklin wouldn't believe and wouldn't accompany him to the temple. But Austin had decided, no matter what he would still go. Alone if needed and give it a shot. He stood up took keys from Franklin and then strolled out of the hospital. He sat in the car and pushed in the ignition key. Just before he started the drive, Franklin walked up and sat in the car. "let's do it for Sara" said Franklin and they both drove off.

This was something that Franklin never believed nor did Austin. But it was the need of the moment and so they went with the flow. After driving the rented car for some time Franklin took the wheel as Austin was still in tears and wasn't comfortable driving. To ensure they don't miss any turn Franklin had put on the GPS which guided them to the temple.

When they neared the temple Austin showed Franklin the location where the accident took place. It was more than twenty-four hours and still the shattered glasses of the bike were lying on the road.

Once they reached Austin got down from the car and ran inside the temple. There was only a bike inside and Austin wasn't comfortable praying to it. But he had come here in a very difficult time and hence joined his hands and begged for Sara's life. Then Franklin came in. He too was shocked to see what Austin was doing. After ten minutes Austin turned around and they both decided to go back to the hospital. Just as they were about to exit the temple, Austin saw the same man, the same employee from the hospital who suggested Austin to visit this temple.

"He's the guy, the same guy from the hospital who asked me to come here" said Austin pointing at him. Franklin couldn't see him, "there he is, standing next to the wall" repeated Austin. "Sorry, I still can't see him," said Franklin. Austin was baffled not knowing what was happening. Austin feared he was hallucinating from the shock of this incident and so he decided to exit from this place as soon as possible.

On their way back, Austin kept thinking if he saw a ghost or was hallucinating. This has never happened to Austin before. But then it paid off. What happened next wasn't anything less than a miracle.

Halfway to the hospital Franklin got a call. It was the call from one of their friends Raj who was at the hospital. Franklin immediately parked the car to the side of the road but was reluctant to answer the call.

Austin and Franklin both feared this call was to inform the worst news that they could hear. But then Austin snatched the phone from Franklin took a deep breath and answered the call. "Hello" said Austin in a sighing voice. Raj replied "Sara's condition is improving. Doctor came in again and checked the reports. There is nothing to fear anymore. Come soon". Austin was again in tears. But these were tears of joy. Franklin asked what did Raj say? "Sara has come back. Raj said her condition has suddenly improved."

Austin didn't believe in psychic or in miracles, but he did now after witnessing one. He apologized to Sara about making fun of her belief and to the 'Bullet Baba'.

Delighted with the news both of them rushed to the hospital to check on Sara and in some time, they reached the hospital.

Austin ran straight to Sara and was even more delighted to see her eyes opened. He hugged her with joy. There was smile on Sara's face but tears in her eyes. After few minutes of sharing their love, the nurse asked everyone to clear the room and only Austin stayed. Then in sometime Sara slept and Franklin walked Austin out of the room to get him to eat something. Austin hadn't consumed food for almost twenty-four hours, and he needed to eat to stay agile. Now Austin had nothing to worry and went alongwith Franklin. On his way he called his brother Franky and updated on Sara's improved condition.

Austin and Franklin had lunch and then went back. After few hours of examining, Sara was shifted from intensive care to a private room where she stayed for another week. She was still undergoing treatment and the doctors regularly monitored her situation. After spending ten days in the hospital, Sara was now out of danger. She was able to talk, walk and more important was able to identify her friends. Doctor had advised her to rest and to avoid any prolonged physical activities and Austin made sure she had no problems whatsoever.

Before going back to Goa, Austin gave away his bike which was repaired now to the temple as a thank you to the 'Bullet Baba' for saving Sara.

After horrendous ten days, they were back home and coincidentally they landed on Sara's birthday. Austin had planned a huge get party for Sara with all her friends but now it was only the few of them. Franklin ordered a cake and they celebrated Sara's birthday with few of the people at home.

Tonight, after a long time, Austin and Sara laid next to each other and talked about the moments to remember from the wedding. From the joyous wedding to the life taking accident, they praised how lucky they were. Then Austin remembered the most important thing that he missed telling Sara.

"I almost forgot to mention you the strangest thing that I witnessed, and I think that maybe the reason you are alive. When I sat next to you at the hospital one guy walked into the room and asked me to visit the temple and offer prayers to the Bullet Baba. Nobody saw him at the hospital, nor did anyone see him walking in the room. At first, I thought this was the reaction to the medication and effect of pain killers. So, I kept it to myself. Then the doctor said you weren't going to make it. At that moment every fiber in my body told me to visit the temple and I thought why not give it a shot. We drove to the temple, offered prayers and when we were walking out of the temple, I again saw what looked like an image of this man. I don't know what that was. If I saw a ghost or if I was hallucinating. But one thing though as soon as we stepped out of the temple, Franklin got call from Raj mentioning your condition improved. This has to mean something right".

Sara was delights to hear it, "Really, you went back to that temple for me. I am glad your mind changed. I think God looks upon us in different forms. May be all of what you witnessed, was a part of it. Best thing is that we are together now".

Then in sometime Sara slept but Austin didn't. The mysterious event involving this guy was reignited in Austin's mind and he kept thinking about it. Austin wanted to cross check again but wasn't sure if going back to Jodhpur was the right thing to do. That place gave him goosebumps and he never wanted to visit it ever again.

Few days went by with business as normal. Austin had taken back the control of his businesses from Franklin and was getting busy day by day. He had initiated few new projects in construction of hospitals and schools. It was like a "Thank You" to the world for saving Sara's life.

Three months had passed now since the accident and the life had become a routine with everything done as per the schedule. Sara being at home was bored out of her mind. Austin realized that and decided to invite all their friends to a party. This was a long-awaited party and this time there was no way it was going to be rescheduled or cancelled. The preparation started and booking arrangements were being discussed. Ten from the group of twenty were available on the scheduled dates and were ready to visit. Franklin and Austin had planned everything, and it all went smoothly. This get together was kept a secret from Sara. It was a surprise party which Austin had in mind for months.

This party was planned at this beach house near Agonda. The plan was to take Sara out for dinner and then turn away to this place where all her friends waited. This place was one of the rarest places that Sara visited and hence was chosen for this surprise party. Austin had renovated this place and the place looked like heaven on earth.

On the big day as per the plan at eight in the evening they were ready. They got in the car and drove to the beach house. Franklin was already at the beach house managing things. As they drove out of the city, Sara asked, 'Where are we going"? and Austin replied "It's a new place near Agonda. We'll reach there in another thirty minutes. It's a beautiful place. One of my friends visited this place and was super impressed" he continued driving.

In another thirty minutes they reached. Sara had suspected something, but she had no idea that she would walk into a beach house and her friends would be waiting on the other side. As she stepped in, Franklin switched on the lights and everyone in the room yelled "Surprise" and boy wasn't she surprised.

Sara was very happy to meet her friends and thanked Austin and Franklin for this memorable evening. After few of hours the party "officially" ended. That night everyone stayed at the beach house. Few slept and for few the after party continued. Next morning, they drove back to their hotel. Everything was organized. Their breakfast and their pickup from the hotel to the airport. Sara and Austin visited the hotel to see them off. Hugs, handshakes, and tears, it was an emotional moment for everyone. These friends were vital part of Sara's life. They all went back at least five years. Austin barely knew them but still he assured his guests were given the farewell they wouldn't complain about. So, he got involved and he too hugged them more as a formality.

Austin had given Sara a time to remember with her friends and now it was Sara's turn to do something similar. She too planned a surprise party next weekend for Austin and invited Franky and his family. It was more of a get together. Franklin was the key for both these surprise parties. He was happy but felt it was getting weird taking turns to surprise each other. Three months since the accident and except office and parties, there was nothing else to worry in Austin life, but then it was Austin's life. There had to be something exciting.

Next evening on his way back from the hotel the unexpected took place. When the car neared the house, something crashed on the car's rear window shattering the glass. Austin was in the back seat but luckily didn't have any serious head injuries. Then the car stopped, and Austin got down. The driver ran to Austin, "aap thik ho sir!" he asked, "yeah, yeah. Im fine. What happened?" asked Austin holding his head. At first, Austin thought a branch fell from the trees but when he saw it was a rock, he suspected an attack. Someone had intentionally thrown it at the car. They both looked around but as it was dark, couldn't see anyone. They both got into the car and drove back home. Austin suspected it could be anyone of his enemies and he had no update on the attackers from the night he met Sara at the Hotel. Kalyan was supposed to take care of that. He called Kalyan and it was time to meet. Austin asked the driver to go home while he turned the car away to another hideout where Kalyan arrived in sometime.

"This is getting out of hands and needs to be taken care of before something bad happens to our family. I expected you to put end to this long ago, did you even find who is behind these attacks," said Austin.

"Yes, some guy named Romeo" replied Kalyan.

This name shook Austin. There were many enemies and Austin never expected Romeo to be behind these attacks. Austin considered Romeo one of his friends and always thought even though they parted ways, they still respected each other. Austin wasn't even sure why Romeo attacked him.

"Do you know him" asked Kalyan.

"Yes, he was a good friend of mine few years ago and reached out to me few times asking for money. This is a something I never saw coming. Talk about trusting people..." Austin was in two minds now, whether to put an end to Romeo or to talk to him and forget about these attacks. But he was too sensitive about the safety of his family and told Kalyan, "Take care of it" and Kalyan replied, "I did, he's gone, I took care of him myself. Ten days ago. I didn't mention it to you as there was a lot going on for you in your personal life" replied Kalyan.

Austin didn't know how to react on this news. He was sad that Romeo was dead "If this wasn't Romeo, then who was it?" asked Austin and they both had nothing to add. Austin got back in his car and drove back home. At first even Kalyan thought it was an accident but then he was Austin's right hand. He got back to finding out who it was.

Austin was restless and had to deal with this anonymous danger before it was too late. So, he called all the cops in his pockets, thieves, drug dealers and everyone denied their part or knowing anyone who were planning an attack on him. All of them knew going up against Austin was like playing with fire.

Couple of days passed and Austin couldn't find anything. Then it happened again and again someone attacked his car in the hotels parking. This time he was not in it. There was a knife pierced in one of the tires with a note on it which said, 'It's time to pay'. Austin was right in suspecting these attacks were intentional and today was just another warning.

Austin believed in finishing his enemy in one shot, so they don't get time to plan a revenge or hide away. But whoever this guy was, he was playing games with Austin, giving Austin time. This scared Austin.

Austin went through the CCTV footage of the parking but didn't see anything fishy. Anyone who hurt Austin didn't got off without paying but this time Austin was helpless. He had spent lot of money and used all his contacts, but nobody knew anything. It was like chasing a ghost. Now Austin realized how the cops felt when they couldn't find the Godless.

Austin was scared because there was threat to the life of people he cared about. When he was alone, he was reckless but now it changed. It was like Batman taking off his cape and letting the world know who he was making him vulnerable to his enemies.

Couple of days passed without any more action and then it was time for the surprise party arranged by Sara. While Austin pursued his hunt for the anonymous attacker, Sara was managing this party. This hunt for the attacker and these attacks were kept from both Sara and Franklin. Sara had got back from a life-threatening injury and Austin didn't want her to worry about family's safety.

Today, it was Saturday morning and Sara had sent one of his drivers to pick Franky and his family at the airport. Their flight was scheduled to land at ten which meant they would be out at the main gate at around eleven and would reach home right on time for a long-awaited family lunch, Just the right surprise for Austin. But as good as it sounded the plan failed when Austin informed Sara that he had to go out for some business and won't be home for lunch. Sara was saddened but as long as he would be surprised to see them later in the day, she was okay with it.

Since their marriage Saturday and Sunday were strictly days to spend with family but today Austin didn't stay home. He was out in search of the person behind that threatening letter and was meeting and threatening his connections he did business with sometime back. To be able to have many more 'Family weekends' he had to work this weekend.

Austin changed his name for a reason. But the change of identity with the same face and in the same place didn't help Austin much. With new name change came a clean slate and many more businesses but couldn't keep all his enemies away. Then he remembered Kalyan's suggestion to move out of Goa which Austin had denied earlier and was now regretting it.

That day, Kalyan had to accompany Austin and so asked him to call in sick to avoid any kind of suspicion. They both drove to the other side of Goa where he met one of his old nemeses, "Rajan".

Austin and Rajan went way back. In fact, one of the first "Drug war" in Goa involved them. Rajan started his carrier making illegal liquors and just like Austin grew into selling drugs. Austin had given him hard time about the division of territory of his business.

Truth be told, Austin had snatched business from Rajan which he had sworn to avenge. As Austin wasn't able to find anyone who intended to harm him recently, he traced back in time and Rajan's name was first on the list.

This meeting between Rajan and Austin could go wrong, it could turn out to be dangerous and so on their way Austin picked up couple of guys as backup. These guys arranged guns in case it was needed. They drove all the way towards to the location informed to Austin by his spies who had spent days tailing Rajan to know his routine. When they reached, Austin was surprised to see Rajan was ready and waiting for him. Austin wasn't aware of the fact that Rajan already knew and was prepared for worst.

"let's not get carried away. I just need answers to some questions. Then I will be on my way" said Austin and made it clear that he had no intentions of a fight. This meeting was just a discussion and both of them agreed to it keep it non-violent.

They both sat in a room and only one person from each side accompanied. Rajan had this huge seven feet tall guy while Austin was supported by Kalyan whose was never going to be threat physically to this giant. Once this giant entered the room Austin and Kalyan were seriously intimidated and hoped to end this meeting without any trouble.

"We want no trouble," said Austin.

Rajan smiled and pointing towards this giant said, "yeah! that is a common response once he walks in".

Austin then suggested that both of their men left the room and only they both talked. Rajan agreed and asked the giant to search Austin from top to bottom. He found a gun which Rajan kept with himself, and Kalyan left the room.

"I have followed you since long and its admirable to see what you have done with the money you made from the business you stole from me. So, what brings a renowned hotelier like you to this side of Goa?" asked Rajan while lighting a cigarette.

"Five years...we haven't crossed our roads in the past five years, and I thought things were in a good place for us, but then there's an attack on me. That's your kind of thing, isn't it?" replied Austin.

"Are you accusing me of coming after you? Look at me. I am way ahead of you, and I don't have time for this. If I want to take you out, I take you out, no questions asked" said Rajan and Austin was somewhat convinced that Rajan had nothing to do with it.

"Well, you better not be the person I am looking for. You know me" said Austin while he took back his gun and walked out of the door. On his way-out Austin stopped and turned around. Rajan was not to be seen and this giant was escorting Austin to his car. That's when, Austin gave his visiting card to this giant and said, "In case you need to upgrade."

On their way back Austin and the guys stopped for lunch at a roadside hotel from where Austin and Kalyan parted their ways.

Austin was frustrated on not being able to end this once and for all. "What to do sir?" asked Kalyan who was driving Austin's car out of the Hotel.

"Who could it be Kalyan. You say Romeo is dead and I don't see anyone else apart from him who is crazy enough to take me on." replied Austin while looking at his gun.

"Maybe someone from the past. Was there anyone whom you might have hurt badly?" asked Kalyan.

"You know my past. There were few but none of them are still alive. Don't you think I wouldn't take care of them?" replied Austin.

Then Austin asked Kalyan to take him to the place where he buried Romeo and Kalyan drove towards Talpona beach. He had buried Romeo in a very small cemetery in a tiny little parish. They reached there in sometime, and the cemetery was behind a Church. Romeo parked the car on side of the road and from there they both walked to the cemetery. They both stood looking at the tombstone and it said, 'A caring person'. "You came up with that?" asked Austin and Romeo nodded yes. "At least you gave him a proper send-off," said Austin and added "You know i knew Romeo and I knew his father. They were the first ones in Goa I became friends with. I have witnessed both of them die and both of them have a special place in my heart. Who knows, if things were better, we would have been friends. May the god rest their souls".

Then with nothing to do and nowhere to go they turned back home. They stopped at Kalyan's place to drop him off and the actual driver to take over.

In another hour at six in the evening Austin reached home. There was nobody around except the maids. "Where is everybody" asked Austin to one of them "they all went on a tour, I heard Sara ma'am asking grandpa to come but he was tired and didn't go, he is resting in his room".

"This was strange. Sara giving a tour! she knew this place in and out. What's with the tour then" Austin said to himself. He then ran upstairs to his room took a bath and came back out on the front lawn for tea. Austin sat at the table while he waited for Sara and Chris to come back. He called her on her cell phone, but it went unanswered. He then waited at the table for tea.

Today was one heck of a day and now it was time to relax. Looking at the lush green mountains and feeling the cold breeze, Austin waited for a hot refreshing tea. In few minutes came a maid with a tray carrying tea and some biscuits for Austin. While he was enjoying them, came another maid with a tray carrying more cups of tea.

"What is this?" he asked.

"It's for Sara ma'am" replied the maid and she left.

Then Austin heard voices of people talking and walking towards the house. It was coming from the backdoor of the lawn. Austin turned around and got up see who it was. First entered Chris and with him was Jonathan. Austin was surprised to see him and then walked in Franky, his wife and Sara. Austin couldn't believe his eyes. He ran towards them and hugged Franky.

"What a surprise. When the maid told me Sara was a giving a tour of this place to someone, I assumed it was her friends. I would have never guessed it to be you guys. Welcome guys. I am so glad you came" Austin responded cheerfully.

"She managed everything. The tickets, our pickup from airport. Thank her" replied Franky pointing to Sara.

They all walked to the table and the maid poured tea for Sara, Franky, and his wife and milk for Chris and Jonathan.

"It's a wonderful place you got here man. I mean I knew you were loaded when you visited my place in a Jaguar but this... this is heaven. A place in the mountains with a view of sunrise and the sunset is something I saw only in the movies and on Television. You are a celebrity Man!" said Franky and once the maid left the table "what's with the maid's man. How many are there?" asked Franky.

"Nine" replied Austin.

"Nine! Humm and it's only you, Sara, and Chris right. So, nine maids to serve two and a half. This is mathematically wrong bro".

On this Austin added, "You also have a maid at home. What's the big deal. "Yeah! but our ratio is one maid to three people, not three maids to one person".

"Let it go. Why are you even talking about maids here" said Franky's wife asking him to change the topic?

Once the snacks were done Austin decided to capture this moment and to frame it. So, he sent one of his servants to arrange a photographer. He came back in an hour at seven thirty in the evenings and Austin asked everyone to get ready for the photoshoot. Austin even called Franklin to be part of it and to spend an evening with them. They had planned a barbeque which was perfect in the cold night of November.

Within couple of hours of meeting his brother Austin had arranged a fun filled evening with the family. Once everyone was all dressed up for the photoshoot, they all gathered in the hall sat on this huge couch and the photographer captured the moment. Franky even took photos with the servants and the maids. Many moments were captured in the expensive camera, but one person was missing, 'Grandpa'. Sara realized it and immediately called for him. Franky hadn't seen him since he got here and wasn't aware who he was. Finally, Grandpa too was part of this family photo, but he wasn't smiling. Didn't look happy. Austin decided to frame that photo and hang it on the wall across the hall.

Then the party moved out of the house to the lawn where barbeque was set. Lights hanging from the trees and soft music had set the mood for dancing and the first ones on the floor were Franky and his wife. Franky was having the time of his life. Something he hadn't done since his college days and so he lived every moment of it. Then joined Austin and Sara.

After dancing for thirty minutes the "couples" took a break. Franklin, Austin, and Sara had whiskey while Franky went for beer. Franky's wife and the kids had fruit juices.

"You must be having lot of parties here right. I mean you must be having many friends over" asked Franky.

"I don't have friends. Only business associates and yes we often spend time drinking and dancing but there are no friends" responded Austin.

"No friends, none?" Franky was surprised.

"I had one but then he left me". Austin was referring to Romeo whom he had considered a friend for some time.

Then as the night went on, first one to call it a night was grandpa. He had dinner and he went to bed. That's when Franky asked "What's the deal with grandpa? who is he? I don't remember him. He is definitely not our blood relative".

"He is the father of someone who worked for me but died in an accident. I took him and his grandson and have been taking care of them since then. He should be in his early sixties. He is very quiet and has hard time hearing. Chris is his grandson." replied Austin while sipping whiskey.

"Yes, Sara told me everything about Chris. I didn't know he was the grandpa. By the way Sara told me everything about your life. How you two met, fell in love, and all about your business and charities. You know what, mom and dad would be proud of what you have achieved and the person you've grown into" Franky was really proud of Austin and didn't hesitate to express it. The fourth bottle of beer helped him speak up.

Then in sometime the kids went to sleep and the ladies took them for bed. Franklin, Franky, and Austin were still up and drinking. They too called it the night in another couple of hours. Franklin stayed the night at the house.

Next morning the kids and the ladies were up early while the men except Franklin, were still down and deep in sleep. Franklin got up early and left the house before anyone noticing it. Vanishing like a morning mist, Franklin did this every time he spend night at Austin's.

Then Franky and Austin got up at ten and met at the table for breakfast. They were the only ones left for breakfast.

"Morning bro, hope you had a good night's sleep" Austin greeted Franky who looked a little itchy.

"Yeah! yeah good morning" replied Franky holding his head.

"Are you okay, what seems to be the issue" asked Austin. He sensed Franky wasn't feeling well.

"My heads spinning, and I feel cramp in my leg. May be from all the beer I drank last night. I must have had too much. Thank god I didn't create scene or vomit anywhere in this beautiful place," said Franky.

With a smile on his face and Austin replied, "you drank only four pints in over six hours bro and not to mention the number of visits to the bathroom. And as far as creating a scene you did one thing. You challenged yourself to run to the mountain as fast as you could,".

"Running to the mountain. That's not bad. It was just my way of releasing adrenaline. Maybe that's why my ankle is in pain" replied Franky.

"Yeah, I agree to that. But... you did it naked" whispered Austin in his ears.

"What? "Asked Franky and added, "Are you sure. Did anyone see me embarrass myself".

"Don't worry. Nobody saw you except me and Franklin. We were the only lucky ones to witness that moment of magic. And by the way, you did vomit. A lot. That eruption is buried outside" added Austin.

They both had a laugh and joined the rest of the family. Then post lunch it was time for the guests to go back. With a promise to meet up soon, Franky, his wife and Jonathan left to the airport where Franklin was waiting to see them off.

"You are good man Franklin, and you have my name. Take care of my family," said Franky. "They are my family too" added Franklin and then they left.

Once Franky and his family left the house felt empty. Austin relaxed while watching sports on television. Chris was playing outdoor with his grandpa and Sara was in the kitchen helping the cooks. In the evening while Austin sat on the lounge in the lawn watching Sunday night football, Grandpa approached him and sat next to him. This was rare and unusual.

Grandpa said, "We know we've had our differences, but I never thanked you for taking me and Chris into your home. Without you, Chris would have landed in a foster home and I...well I might have been washed away in some gutter".

Austin looked at him and replied "don't say that. When God closes one door, he opens another one".

"Yeah, god does that it seems. By the way who is the family that we had over today" asked Grandpa.

"Everything" replied Austin.

"Okay I'll leave you to your game. Nice talking to you" grandpa got up and left.

"Yeah, nice talking to you grandpa...for the first time" replied Austin sarcastically and got back to watching his game. He assumed Grandpa didn't hear him, but he did.

Next morning it was business as usual. Austin on his way to manage his business, Chris to school, Sara back to being a housewife. On his way Austin remembered the unusual conversation that he had with grandpa and so he stopped at the tea stall. He got down from the car and walked to the stall. It was a mess. Austin never liked this tea stall as it spoiled the beauty around his house. He only allowed it as he felt guilty for what had happened to grandpa's family. This stall was now a breeding place for insects and mosquitos and smelled really bad…really…really bad. He decided to tear it down and may be built something else…something like a gazebo. After all this place had the view of all the mountains and would be a pleasant place to chill. He immediately called Kalyan and asked him to demolish this stall and invite quotations for the building of gazebo. Then he sat in the car and left.

Austin always included himself into something that kept him busy and this time it was the gazebo. That day till the time he got back home in the evening there were photos and designs on the table for Austin to go through and approve. Austin approved a gazebo which could seat eight people minimum and post finalizing the budget the work began.

Next morning the tea stall was being demolished by an excavator. There were many things in it that belonged to grandpa, but it was now turned into pieces. Eight hours for six straight days and building Gazebo was completed. It looked awesome and the view from there was unbelievable. The honour of inaugurating this place was given to Franky and it was arranged the coming weekend. On the other hand, Grandpa was still in the dark. He wasn't aware that tea stall had been demolished. Nobody bothered to tell him. Grandpa barely visited it since Austin sheltered him in his house and maybe that's why Austin took this step without informing Grandpa.

It was now Saturday. Franky and his family were on their way to Austin's house. Franky couldn't sleep the night. He was too excited to visit his brother. They were supposed to reach the house till ten and they weren't the only guests. Austin had invited few of his friends but mostly the member of the board and the managing committee to this inauguration party. Franky had no clue what was in store for him. It was a surprise!

Austin didn't go to airport to pick up Franky. He sent a car instead. Franky and his family arrived on time and on the way, they noticed the gazebo and asked the driver about it who denied knowing anything.

"Freshen up and be ready guys. I have a surprise for you" said Austin and greeted Franky and his family to his house. Austin went back to the Gazebo to manage the guests while Franklin escorted everyone from the house to Gazebo. Grandpa was surprised of them all.

"What happened to my tea shop?' he asked and there was no reply from anyone. This made him sad as he didn't even get to say goodbye or collect his things. Grandpa had a connection with this place which nobody thought of before shattering it down to dust.

At the gazebo, soft music was playing while the guests enjoyed their snacks. They were all talking to each other but mostly about business. Then reached Franky and his family. Austin had the centre stage and invited them up to the gazebo.

"May I have your attention please. Everyone I'd like you to meet my Family. My Brother Franky, his son

Jonathan, and his wife Maria. They are here today on this special occasion as we inaugurate this new monument" said Austin while handing a scissor to his brother and asking him to cut the ribbon.

Few people at the party were confused. Building a gazebo was just another renovation at Austin's house. The need to throw a party and calling these many people wasn't clear. Everyone including Franklin and even Franky waited to hear what Austin had to say.

There was a huge round of applause once the ribbon was cut and when it stopped Austin took the stage.

"Thanks guys but this is not the only reason why you all are here. I know your time is precious and I don't intent to waste it. The real reason is this". Austin was holding a file in his right hand, and it was obvious that the documents inside the file had something to do with the announcement. "Many of you at some point in my life, asked me where my family is. Well, here it is now. Today my Family is complete and that is why I announce a change in the leadership".

Everyone was shocked and eagerly waiting to hear what the change was. Austin had specifically invited his investors, lawyers, and board to this meeting as this change was in a way going to impact them.

"Starting today all of my business except the hotel will be managed by Franky. He is your new managing director". This announcement shocked everyone. There was silence and tension in the air.

Apart from the hotel, Austin owned few chains of coffee outlets, few insurance companies and as Franky background was in finance, he seemed a suitable candidate. This was a shocker of news for everyone. Austin wanted Franky to be part of his legacy, but it backfired.

"What is going on? let's talk about it first. I am not ready for it, and I am surprised you decided without discussing it with me" reacted Franky and rushed back to the house with his family.

This situation immediately changed and as the music was also stopped for the announcement, the silence made it more awkward. Austin was speechless while all the eyes were dead straight on him. Although Austin had the controlling interest in the companies, "The Board" was not the people to be messed with. With an assurance to handle this situation and to come back with the confirmation in few days, Austin ran back to the house with Sara and Chris to talk to Franky.

The music stopped and the party died. Gazebo emptied in another fifteen minutes. Everyone left. Everyone but grandpa who was sitting in the corner…completed unnoticed. Grandpa then walked up to the gazebo and sat there for some time with tears in his eyes. After an hour a car came to pick him up. When he reached home, everyone was having lunch. Grandpa was the last one to join and the last one left at the table. He was heartbroken and wanted to talk to someone, but he had nobody to talk to.

Franklin noticed everything and he asked Sara if she knew about this change of title. She confirmed that it was something they both discussed but she wasn't aware about this announcement.

"Austin shouldn't have announced it the way he did. He should have first spoken to Franky and his colleagues and only when they agreed...this change should have been announced," said Sara.

That afternoon there was awkward silence in the house and when Austin approached Franky to talk about it, Franky denied any discussion on it. Franky was now in his room with his wife. Austin was in his room with Sara. Grandpa in his room probably in tears and Franklin was babysitting both Chris and Jonathan. It was a rare moment of sadness in this house.

After an hour both the couples walked out of their rooms. One from the right and other from the left. Coincidently at the same time. Franklin saw them. It was like a scene from a television drama series that nobody watches. Ironically everything happening in this house in the last few days was nothing short of a script from a television series. This one was extremely interesting though.

Franky and Austin sat at the table and talked about it for some time. It was concluded that this offer was too much for Franky and he needed lot of time to prepare himself for it. He didn't actually decline this offer but requested to keep it on hold for couple of years. Austin agreed and this topic was off the table for the rest of the weekend.

In some time, things were back to normal. Guys getting drunk, kids playing and the ladies talking about ladies' stuff. Party every weekend was the new normal here.

Franklin and Kalyan stayed back at the house post celebration. Next morning Franklin dropped Kalyan to his house while he drove away to his. They had to come back Monday morning and had the rest of the Sunday for themselves.

At the house the routine started with breakfast. Then playing few indoor and outdoor games, few beers for Franky and then off to the airport. Austin's house had become a favourite weekend gateway for Franky and his family. Both the families enjoyed their time together and already made plans for the coming weekend. A picnic at the beach.

After the fun filled weekend, it was now Monday or as some say, 'End of fun day'. Austin and Sara woke up as per their schedule and post the morning walk, they waited at the table for breakfast which was served in the next ten minutes. Then it was time to get going. Just then Austin realized that he hadn't seen Kalyan since morning. That was unusual. He's always there at the house right on time. Assuming Kalyan might have been at another late-night party last night and might still be sleeping, Austin didn't call and was on his way.

Franklin was at the hotel on time and then it was business all day which wasn't easy after the stunt Austin pulled this past weekend. The out of the blue announcement of a 'Slumdog becoming a millionaire' had got him in trouble with the investors and the board.

Many of his partners and investors weren't in favour of it. For them it was a stab in the back. Austin's first half of the day included calming the pissed off investors, board members and partners. He understood from their responses that things were never going to be easy for him in the long run. Finally at four Austin spoke to each one of them, explained them the situation and gained their trust back. By then he realized that he made a huge mistake by "Going with the flow". This mantra helped him in his life earlier, but not this time.

By four, Austin was exhausted and called it a day. Chris was at school and Sara at home. Austin decided to go home with bunch of movies and surprise Sara. It had been long since Sara and Austin spent time watching a movie marathon and desperately remembered their time at the farmhouse in Panvel.

All excited Austin asked his driver to take him to the nearest shop with latest movies. He picked up few action movies and was on his way when he got a call on his cell phone. It was from one of the cops that was close to him. Austin was a little surprised to get a call from him. He answered, "Hello". The cop on the other end was Xavier, a corrupt cop, the one in Austin's pocket and payroll.

"Sir, I'm sorry its bad news. Kalyan is dead," said Xavier.

"What" asked Austin, "are you out of your mind. What are you saying" yelled Austin to the cop.?

"Sir, I am telling the truth. I'm at his house. He's dead in front of me" replied Xavier.

"I am coming there" Austin asked the driver to take him to Kalyan's house.

When Austin reached Kalyan's house, he met Xavier and covered in the blanket was the body of Kalyan. Austin couldn't believe it.

"What happened? "Asked Austin.

"He was strangled" replied Xavier.

It was a murder and Austin was furious and sad for losing a close friend. Austin asked Xavier to keep him updated on the investigation and then he left the crime scene.

Austin was scared. There were already few attempts on his car which were meant for him and now this. He knew someone was onto him, but he was helpless not knowing who it was and now that Kalyan was dead, the chances of finding it out faded. But Austin wasn't going to just sit around and do nothing. He took drastic steps and the first one was the increased security at home. On the other hand, his search for the murderer grew more extensively. He called up every damn cop and politician whom he paid and threatened them to find the killer. As the day passed, the news of Kalyan's murder had now reached to everyone of their family members and friends and even back in Mumbai to Franky.

Sara and Austin stayed home for the next couple of days. As Franklin was the last one to see Kalyan alive, he was brought in for questioning by the cops. Once the cops were done questioning Franklin, the cops brought in Austin and Sara. The cops even got hold of Franky and his wife back in Mumbai. All their stories checked out and the cops couldn't find the motive linking anyone of them to Kalyan's murder. They were no longer the suspect and were let go. Sara wasn't pleased with all of it and knew one day something serious like this would happen.

Meanwhile, in Mumbai, Franky was terrified of the interrogation and as soon as the Mumbai police let him and his family go, he called Austin to understand what had happened. Austin told Franky that the cops found Kalyan's body at his house. There was nothing else to add so Austin hung up.

Austin had to get to the bottom of this, he had to find the killer. Kalyan was his buddy and had been with him through good times and bad. His absence had certainly left a hole in Austin's life. There was only one thing on his mind now to avenge Kalyan's murder.

Austin's follow up with the cops increased. He was like a hungry lion wanting to kill. This news spread to everyone who knew Austin and his nemesis from the dark side of the society offered him help. But as Austin didn't trust anyone of them, he rejected. Not only did he reject their offer, but he threatened them. This did nothing but increase the number of people wanting to hurt Austin. This event brought the worst out of Austin and his behaviour changed severely. He drank too much of alcohol, got into fights with the cops and sometimes even with Sara. The atmosphere at home was something that Franklin had never seen before since he was with Austin. Even Sara expressed this concern. They tried to speak to Austin, but he didn't listen. That's when Sara thought of asking Franky to talk to Austin. Maybe Franky could help.

Post discussing with Sara Franky wanted to talk to Austin to calm him down. He called Austin many times, but Austin never answered the call. Franky feared he might lose Austin again and so he decided to visit Austin and talk to him face to face. Next morning Franky took his car and was on his way to Goa. He decided to stay for the night and leave the next morning.

Five days had passed since the murder and so far, the cops didn't have a single clue. This matter got escalated to topmost officials, but nothing moved. Austin put pressure on the cops again using his contacts at high places but all he got was assurances. Sara was a private investigator sometime back and was still in contacts with many people who helped her solve cases earlier. She spoke to them, and they all offered to help.

The next day Franky was at Austin's place at three in the afternoon and he couldn't believe how badly Austin had taken the death of Kalyan. Franky didn't know Austin and Kalyan were so close …well he didn't know the past. Franky spoke to Austin, and he calmed him down. Austin was not only grieving Kalyan's death but was also worried about the safety of his family. Franky didn't know that.

That evening everyone in the house sat together for dinner. Even the maids and servants joined. Franky talked to everyone about Kalyan's death and assured their safety. He also promised to find Kalyan's killer and to put him behind the bars. Franky was close to the servants at Austin's house and suggested they all pray for the Kalyan's soul to rest in peace. Then they all had dinner, and everyone went to their rooms. Franky was tired from the eight-hour drive and as he had to leave at six in the morning, he went to bed early.

Next morning Sara, Austin and Franky were up at five. Sara made breakfast for Franky, and he was on his way. Seeing off Franky, Sara and Austin went back to sleep. Then in an hour, one servant came calling and knocked rigorously on their door. He came rushing in with the worse news, "Your bother met with an accident. His car crashed a tree on his way down."

Austin and Sara immediately ran down and, on the way, called for ambulance and the cops. When they reached the site, Franky was inside the car, breathing but unconscious. The car crashed into the trees pretty hard damaging the entire front side and some part inside the car. It looked like Franky was over speeding on this steep road downhill and lost control. In the next thirty minutes, ambulance reached the site and prepared pulling Franky out of the car. Then arrived the cops and an excavator to pull the car out. Franky was now pulled out of the car and taken straight to the hospital. Austin and Sara accompanied him in the ambulance. Car was taken to the police station for logging an accident complaint, verifying insurance and for finding out the root cause. This was insisted by Austin. He suspected this was not an accident.

On the way Austin called Franklin and asked him to visit the hospital. Then Sara called Franky's wife and asked her to come as early as possible.

With multiple internal and head injuries, Franky had lost lot of blood in the car and on his way to the hospital. At the hospital he was taken to the critical care unit where post bandaging the wounds and doses of medicines the doctor kept him under monitoring.

In the next few hours Maria and Jonathan reached the airport. Franklin picked them up and brought them to the hospital.

Franky was kept in the intensive care unit and was fighting for his life. This reminded Austin the horrendous time when Sara was in the same situation fighting for her life. That moment Austin was even considering a visit to the miraculous temple in Jodhpur which he believed brought Sara back to life. But he had to be there by his brother's side. He urged everyone in the family and friends to pray to God for Franky's life.

Everyone from the house including the servants were at the hospital. Everyone except the grandpa. Not sure if he was even aware of this incident. Everyone prayed to God to bring Franky back and in few hours their prayers were answered.

Franky's condition improved he had opened his eyes. But nobody was allowed to talk to him. Austin met the doctors who had checked up on Franky and as per them there was progress. Franky wasn't out of danger yet and the doctors continued to monitor his heath.

In the next few hours Franky asked for his wife and son. They were allowed to meet Franky, and they entered the room. They came out after ten minutes and then Austin was called for. In sometime Austin came out and then nobody was allowed to meet Franky. Austin was bemused when he came out of the room. He didn't speak to anyone. Franklin noticed that but he didn't talk about it at the hospital.

In sometime Austin sent Sara, Maria, and Jonathan back home to get some rest while he stayed at the hospital. Franklin stayed with Austin for some time but then he too went home. Austin sat next to Franky and in some time he fell asleep.

Next morning Austin woke up when the nurse walked in to check on Franky. While the nurse checked up on Franky, Austin walked out to the washroom to freshen up. On his way back he saw doctors and nurses rushing in the ICU to check on Franky. He got scared and ran towards Franky. All the nurses were preparing to take him to other room.

"what's going on? Can someone please tell me where you are taking him" asked Austin with fear in his voice.

"Franky needs a surgery. His condition worsened" replied the doctor and they carried him to operation theatre.

Austin was scared. He had no idea what was happening, and nobody talked to him either to explain what was going on. He immediately called Sara and asked her to bring Maria to the hospital as early as possible. Sara and Maria reached hospital in another forty-five minutes but by then it was too late. Franky was declared dead.

As per the doctors, due to internal injuries and loss of blood, Franky's body couldn't react positively to the medicines and his body refused the fight.

This news shattered the entire family. Sara and Franklin were the ones front ending and taking care of things at the hospital. Sara was taking care of Maria while Franklin was with Austin this whole time. Kids were at home with Grandpa.

After few hours doctors released the body to be taken home. Funeral was arranged the next morning at the church. Initially Franky's wife wanted to take the body back to Mumbai but then she changed her mind and agreed for cremation here in Goa. Post the sermon at the church, Franky's body was brought back home as it was to be buried in the backyard of Austin's house. This was Austin's request to bury Franky in this huge open land rather than a cemetery. He wanted to stay close to Franky.

After the funeral Maria and Jonathan went back to Mumbai and never visited Austin's house again. Austin never met them in his life. Sara was in touch for some time but when she sensed Maria didn't want her in their life, she left them alone. In few weeks' time things were getting back to normal. Austin involved himself with managing the business and Sara got back to managing the house.

Austin still followed up with the cops and Sara with her contacts but there was no progress. Austin's was going crazy, and his mind was fiddling with him. He suspected someone from his office might have been responsible for Franky's death after all he was going to take over the business. He talked to the cop in charge Mr Goel and they both spoke to each one of them with a possible motive but post their interrogation nothing much could be concluded. This only resulted into them holding grudge against Austin for insulting them.

One Saturday afternoon, while Austin was going through family photos on his laptop, he suddenly remembered what Franky told him when he visited him in the ICU. Austin had forgotten about it earlier but now it struck him, and he immediately called in Franklin to talk about it. Franklin got there as early as he could.

"Come on in. I forgot to tell you something extremely importance. Something that is bothering me," said Austin.

"What is it" asked Franklin.

"Remember when Franky was conscious at the hospital, and I spoke to him in the ICU. Well, he told me that he suspected someone had messed up with the brakes of the car and the seatbelt. It was functioning perfectly normal till he reached home. He told me that, the brakes weren't functioning, and the seatbelt was stuck. He couldn't control the speed of the car, nor could he jump out. Franky felt this was done on purpose. Someone had messed up with the car that night. This means the killer was in our house that night and waited for this moment. I don't know how I missed that for so many days. Do you think this can help narrow down the search?"

Franklin wasn't convinced, "Well for starters, the cops have already spoken to the staff, and everyone loved Franky. Except the staff, it was only you guys at the house. Don't you think it could really be a problem with the car. The brakes failed and the seatbelt was really stuck. If this was a murder, the cops would have found something, but they didn't. Not even the fingerprints. This search is going on for days and still there is not a single clue. I know this is driving you crazy and you are suspecting everyone is the killer. But this could really be an accident".

"Think my friend...think. First Kalyan's murder and now this. Don't you feel something's wrong here. I mean many people knew that in few months Franky was going to be the sole owner of many businesses and maybe someone got to him before Franky could take over. Wait a minute. What about you. How could you not have the motive to do this?".

Austin even suspected Franklin to be the killer. He had the motive to take out the competition. After all he was with Austin since long and was already managing this business for Austin.

"So, this is what it has come to. After all this time you think I killed your brother, who...by the way was a brother to me too. You do what you want but I didn't do it. I would never think of hurting a gem of a person like Franky" replied Franklin with uncertainty in his voice.

Franklin knew Austin wasn't in the right state of mind and so he didn't leave his side. He stayed with him like his brother would have done.

Austin had a point. But it was just a theory until proven otherwise. Now that Austin suspected Franky's accident could be a murder, he was out of his mind. Two unsolved murders of his close ones was driving him crazy.

Sadly, this two weren't the only issues Austin was concerned about. Someone was trying to sabotage everything that Austin had accomplished. His personal and professional life was shattered and few days into this chaos, Sara received an envelope with "Truth" written on it and the sender's name was Romeo.

While shadowing Austin for years, he collected many concrete evidence against Austin. Evidence about his illegal past and all the wrong that he had done. There were photos of contracts that he won by bribing officials and the cops, call recordings of ordering hit on people, statement of victims, photos showing his involvement in drugs deals and bank heists. It even had the mention about his safe houses across india. It turned out Romeo was blackmailing Austin into extorting money from him, but Austin didn't take him seriously. This evidence was strong enough to put Austin away for minimum of twenty years. Austin knew that but was blinded by all the money and power he had. He didn't see this move and it came back to bite him.

Kalyan claimed that he had taken care of Romeo then who sent these to Sara? Was Romeo still alive? Was he responsible for the death of Kalyan and Franky? Austin was stunned.

On receiving this envelope Sara knew Austin's end was nearing and she thought about it a lot. Then decided to stay away from him. All this time it was like a lamb sleeping with the lion. Sara now knew it could come back to her and she left him instantly. Sara didn't even leave a note she just placed this envelope on the bed for Austin to know that she knew about it and that she wasn't coming back.

That evening when Austin came back home, he went straight to the bedroom to talk to Sara. Instead saw this envelope on the bed. He opened it and it shook the ground beneath his feet. He knew that Sara had seen it and he suspected she must have left. He asked around in the house and the servants confirmed that she left with huge bag. Austin tried calling her on her cell phone but there was no response. He even asked the cops to trace her cell phone which they did. Last time her cell phone was switched on was on the way to the railway station and then it was switched off.

Austin then called Franklin to his home and explained him the situation. Austin asked him If he knew where Sara could go. Franklin had no clue. Franklin knew the hangout of Sara's friends and met them, but nobody knew anything, nor had they spoken to her in months. Austin had no other option but to register a legal complaint with the cops but before that he had to get rid of all the evidence that was lying there on the bed. He burned that envelope and made the call. Austin assumed that by registering a legal complaint there would be less fingers pointing at him but as the history dictates, the husband is always the first suspect in case the wife goes missing. In this case Franklin was the witness on Austin's side.

Austin and Franklin went out in search of Sara and came home without any information. Next morning Austin got up and as per his normal routine went to get ready. He had forgotten that Sara had left but then it stuck him. He immediately ran out to check if Sara was back but to his surprise the entire house was empty. All the servants had left and there was no sign of Grandpa and Chris either. Austin looked around the house and in the backyard. But nobody was to be seen. It was strange that everyone left him in the night without even talking to him.

When he came to Goa, in his early days, he had nobody. As his life went on, he made many friends who also became his family. Austin's house was filled with family and friends but today he stood in the same house with no family and no friends. Austin was all alone and helpless. It was too much for him to take and to he decided to stay away from the world. He locked himself at home and drowned himself into the sorry ocean of alcohol. He didn't even open door for Franklin who was managing the business and regularly checked up on Austin. Austin was a powerful man with all the money but was powerless without a family.

A week passed and nobody had seen Austin. He was still locked at home. As Austin wasn't answering any calls, the cops decided to pay him a visit at his home that weekend. They had few questions on Sara's disappearance.

Next morning the cops were at Austin's house. The main gate was open and there were no guards around. They rang the bell many times, but nobody answered. There was nobody to open the door.

"Austin, can you hear us? We called you many times. But you didn't answer. We have some questions about the disappearance of your wife. It will take only few minutes. If you can hear us, please open the door" called out one of the cops.

In the next five minutes the door opened. The cops were the first ones to see Austin in person since he had locked himself in the house. His appearance had changed. He had a beard and was stinking badly of alcohol.

"Can we come in?" asked the cop. Austin looked at them, there were three and allowed only their boss to step in. Austin knew most of the cops but didn't recognize their leader. He was new in town but then Austin got back to his senses as soon as he heard this cops name.

"I am Mr Bhatnagar and now I am in charge. I understand this is a difficult time for you and we appreciate you allowing us to talk to you. We are investigating the disappearance of you wife Sara and had few questions," introduced Mr Bhatnagar.

Mr Bhatnagar was the super cop who failed in catching Godless years ago. His return passed a shiver thought Austin's body, but he wasn't scared. He knew Mr Bhatnagar had nothing on him in the past and nothing on him even today.

"It's not a disappearance when someone walks out on you. She left me and if you don't have any update about her whereabouts, I have nothing to say. By the way where is Mr Goel. He was the one in charge right" replied Austin.

"Don't know. I am in charge now and so far; we have nothing that could help us track Sara. But we know that she took a train to somewhere. We have alerted all the railway cops and released her photo" added Mr Bhatnagar.

"You never have any information. I wonder how you are still a cop. Good for nothing" Austin said to himself and then replied, "You have no information about Sara, no clue who killed Kalyan and you don't even have any analysis that my brother didn't die of accident. When can we trust the cops to bring justice? Anyways, talk. What do you want to know?" asked Austin.

"We need details of all the people Sara knew. Her friends and family and all your houses. Legal and Illegal."

"There is nothing I can help with; you may please close the door on your way out" replied Austin as he stood up to go back to his drinking.

"You know we are not super humans with magical power. We need to rely on the information that we collect from our sources and from people like you. This search will only delay If you don't help" replied Mr Bhatnagar. He then stood up, turned around and walked towards the door that's when he saw that family photo. He took it down and asked, "who are they, can you tell me their names and addresses. Maybe they can help."

Austin took the photo from his hands, "let's see who can help. This first one is Franklin who is my assistant and like me has no idea. Then this is Sara, the one you are searching for. This one is my brother who is dead, and you still believe it was an accident, she is his wife who is in Mumbai along with her son and away from us. This is Chris and this is his grandfather who I have no idea where they are. I am sure your team has already spoken to all of them. Tell me who can help from these?' asked Austin.

"Who is this grandpa and why isn't there any mention about him in any reports. Information available with me doesn't mention anything about your grandpa or Chris. Who are they" asked Mr Bhatnagar?

"They are someone I took in when their family died. Chris is too young to understand things and Grandpa is too old to even hear things. He is good for nothing and surely can't help" replied Austin.

Mr Bhatnagar then took out his cell phone and looked at one photo, "It's not clear, but matches this guy... maybe fifty percent," said Mr Bhatnagar.

"Who is he and why are we seeing it" asked confused Austin.

"One of the camera's picked him up on a road leading to Kalyan's house," said the cop.

"So, what! there are so many people walking on that road daily. This could be anyone. What is so special about it" asked Austin.

"You are right it could be anyone. But this man was walking straight, perfectly as young man when he walked in, but when he returned, he hobbled. We suspect he knows something."

"This is great that you guys have managed to pick up such minute details. But grandpa could barely lift himself from the bed. No way he could be that guy in the photo. I am sorry to say but I think you are shaking the wrong tree" Austin still didn't believe the cops theory.

"Where is he anyways. I need to talk to him" asked Mr Bhatnagar.

"I can't find him, and I don't care. The only reason I invited him into my house was because Sara. And now that she is gone, I just don't care" replied Austin and got back to drinking.

Mr Bhatnagar thanked Austin for his time and gave Austin his contact to reach in case he had an update on grandpa and then they left.

The cop, Mr Bhatnagar was pretty sure that grandpa had something to do with it, but Austin was least bothered knowing it could never be this old man. He then locked the door from inside and got back to his drinking.

Next morning once Austin's hangover was gone, he went through few of the old photos that he had. While Sara and Franky's photos brought tears to his eyes, a photo of grandpa few years younger with his tea stall alerted him. Grandpa's face was clear in this photo and so he decided to hand it over to the cop. Austin still didn't believe that Grandpa could do any of these things, but his conscious suggested him to visit the cops and deliver this photo.

Austin stepped out of the house after a week and went straight to the police station and asked for Mr Bhatnagar. He wasn't available and was out on rounds. Austin didn't just visit the cops to handover the photo, he also wanted to help the cops in finding the person behind Kalyan's and his brother murder and so went in with an intent to fully cooperate. Austin waited at the station and in an hour walked in Mr Bhatnagar. He saw Austin waiting on the bench and asked his constable to send him in his office.

"Look what the cat dragged in" said Mr Bhatnagar and added, "to what do I owe this pleasure."

"I came to give you this. It's a photo of grandpa. Clearer one from months ago. May be this can help you find him," said Austin.

"You know what, you all always blame the cops for not being effective and not being fast enough. For your information we got them" Mr Bhatnagar had a smile on his face.

"Got who? Kalyan's killer? Or Franky murderer? or Sara? Whom did you find" asked Austin sarcastically?

"Being a smart ass huh. We got this grandpa and his grandson. Grandpa is in the interrogation room and Chris is it...he is in other room having some snacks." replied Mr Bhatnagar.

"Great, you found the ones I wasn't searching for. Anyways where and how did you find them" replied Austin.

"At the railway station trying to run away. It was the presence of the kid that made it possible to track him so quickly. Anyways I am walking in for questioning now. You can look through the glass" added Mr Bhatnagar and Austin agreed.

Austin walked into a room and through a huge glass saw grandpa and Mr Bhatnagar sitting in the room. Austin had never been on this side of the room but was surely on the other side being interrogated. Normally there are two cops playing a "Good cop, Bad cop" routine but today there was only one.

Mr Bhatnagar had been labelled a super cop back in the day and was posted in Goa for the second time. So far Austin wasn't impressed. In his years of service, Mr Bhatnagar only managed to get rid of a famous hitman in Mumbai whose body was never found. That hitman was termed missing and not dead. And because of his failed history, Austin had no hopes of finding his brothers and Kalyan's murderers.

"Do you know them?" Mr Bhatnagar placed few photos of Austin, Sara, Franky, and Franklin on the table for grandpa to recognize. Grandpa saw them but didn't respond. The cop asked again and again there was no response. Then he showed the family photo where grandpa was seen with them. There was change of expression on grandpa's face, but he was still silent.

Grandpa looked like a tough nut to track, and Mr Bhatnagar got a glimpse of it. He could have easily opted for harsh methods, but he kept his cool. On the other hand, Austin thought grandpa didn't react because he couldn't hear Mr Bhatnagar. So, he told to the cops next to him, "He has hard time hearing. Your boss will have to raise his voice".

Mr Bhatnagar starred at grandpa for some time and grandpa starred back. There was awful silence, and the hell was about to break loose. Austin wasn't sure what Mr Bhatnagar's next move was but then came the trump card. Grandpa's history and it was unbelievable.

As per Mr Bhatnagar, in 1980s, grandpa was the most prolific hitman with more than hundred kills to his name. It was the time when Mumbai was becoming the underworld of India. Grandpa was singlehandedly responsible for the activities of the mafias and drug lords. He did anything for money and could never be trusted. Ruthless and cunning, he had an history of backstabbing his own people for money. Cops tried to get to him for years, but they could never get near him and then he vanished from the face of the earth He was assumed he was dead. Mr Bhatnagar was leading that investigation and took the credit of getting rid of

"Jaggu". This was the same guy Mr Bhatnagar claimed was taken care of but here he was. Grandpa was Jaggu.

Austin couldn't believe his ears. Grandpa a Hitman. This was even bigger than Austin's secret and it scared the crap out of Austin.

One thing which impressed Austin was the fact that even though Mr Bhatnagar assured the world that Jaggu would never return, he never stopped looking for him. His years of perseverance finally paid off. Then Mr Bhatnagar said that he has demanded his transfer back to Goa when he was tipped off by one of his informants about the presence of Jaggu. He identified Jaggu by the tattoo of a gun on his left ankle which became famous in the 80s. Austin thought Mr Bhatnagar was good for nothing, but he did catch the one he was after for years. That's determination. On the other hand, if whatever he said was true, it's possible that grandpa might have been behind Kalyan's murder. But then the question was why…why would he do it?

Unveiling of this dark secret, got him talking. Grandpa admitted that he's the one who killed Kalyan and started venting out.

"I had to move out of Mumbai as Mumbai wasn't safe. On one hand, the cops were chasing me like rabid dogs and on the other hand, my enemies tried many attacks to kill me. I had to move out and there was no better place than Goa.

When I came to Goa, I lived a quiet life to stay away from any limelight that could get me in trouble. I took a job at a small hotel where I met a girl. We fell in love got married and had a kid. Life was going well. When my kid grew, he was started working for Austin. That's where he met his wife and then they had a kid. Life was good for all of us until Austin killed my son and his wife. He arranged Kalyan to kill them and made it look like an accident. That's when I decided to avenge their death. I waited for long time for the right time. I wanted him to feel the pain of losing a family. A family for a family. But when I got to know there was no one that he cared about, killing him wasn't the revenge I was planning. So, I built a tea stall near his home to track his life. Every man settles at some point in their life, and I waited for Austin's life to take a turn and it did. He had a wife and a brother who became his world and that's when i decided to take them away from him.

Romeo was an old enemy of Austin and "Enemy's enemy is a friend" right. So, we came together to destroy Austin. I helped Romeo collect evidence against Austin who had no clue about it. Austin assumed changing his name and getting rid of few enemies would keep him safe. Romeo couldn't stand Austin's success and was in a hurry to eliminate him, but I told him to wait for the right moment. Romeo was hot-headed and he went behind my back and attacked Austin few times. That cost him his life. But I waited. I waited for the right moment. And when Austin was the happiest in his life, I went after his happiness. I got to Kalyan first as he was Austin's right hand and the one who actually killed my family. Once the dangerous Kalyan was out of the way it was easy for me. My next target was Sara but then Franky came into picture. So, I messed with the brakes and his seatbelt knowing it would be difficult to stop an out-of-control speeding car driving downhill. When the car crashed, I was there. He was alive and had seen me there. I had to ensure he died which I did at the hospital slipping him untraceable poison which stopped his heart. Sara was the only person in that house who cared about me. I had second thoughts about killing her and instead I sent her the photos and evidence about Austin's life she wasn't aware of. And then as expected she took off when she got to know who Austin really was.

Austin biggest crime was when he took away my grandson against my will. He was the only reason I wanted to stay alive. Austin took away my family and I did the same to him. Only difference is he did it for money and I did it for my son. Austin always thought money outlasts respect and he was wrong. I have also sent those evidence against Austin to you and I know Austin is standing behind that glass. So do it. Go on and arrest him"

Austin was blown away from what he heard. The cops looked at Austin with disbelief. This was the end of Austin and his reign as the boss of Goa. After all these years of getting away, finally the cops had something to charge him with.

As merciless as grandpa was as a hitman, he was softened by love in his new life. Now that he confessed to killing Kalyan and Franky, he knew he had to spend the rest of his life in jail, and he wasn't ready to do it. "Take care of Chris" he said and then pulled out the gun from Mr Bhatnagar's belt and shot himself. Grandpa died on the spot. The cops then arrested Austin based on the evidence sent by grandpa.

Mr Bhatnagar finally had his hands on Godless. Today was the best day in Mr Bhatnagar's life. His journey as a cop ended and he announced his retirement in few days, but his legacy as super cop continued.

At the trial, this evidence didn't link Austin to anything serious. He was guilty of petty crimes like bribing or running illegal things. Nothing traced back to Austin and so he was jailed only for five years. There was no proof that Austin was behind the death of Grandpa's son. It seemed like Grandpa's revenge got the wrong people. Austin wasn't charged directly for any homicide and hence didn't get sentence for life. He was lucky to see things go his way…again.

All the time in the jail Austin looked back on the deeds that brought his life to an end. He rotted in jail and all the money and power that he had acquired wasn't valuable anymore. It was all for nothing. He blamed himself for the death of his brother who was survived by a son and wife. Their life was never the same and only Austin was to blame. He still missed Sara and hoped she was alive and safe. He also missed Chris who was taken away to a foster home.

The first five months were difficult for him to adapt to the life in jail. He was attacked many times and many times he tried to kill himself but every time the guards saved him. Even the cops on Austin's payroll went down with him for their involvement in all the illegal activities that he was part of. He was living in hell.

There were hundreds of convicts in the jail all serving time and to make them a better man, the jailer arranged few therapy sessions every fortnight. It was like a group session where some famous psychologist or priests came in a spoke to them about forgiveness, kindness, about God and humanity. This was arranged particularly so that the people here would change and live a better life when they got out. Whoever attended it were in peace.

Austin was still suffering from the guilt of being responsible for many deaths and hence his cellmate insisted he attended these session's. He hesitated at first but then he agreed. It was hosted by a priest, and he spoke about how one can forgive themselves, embrace the spirit and let the healing begin. First session Austin attended left him amazed. He soon grew into it and as per the priest's guidance he steered his life. Every time a different priest came in and they all taught different ways on how people can change the way they looked at life and adapt new things that took them closer to almighty. 'Healing' was getting close to the god and feeling his presence among them.

During his time in jail Austin had only one visitor, Franklin. Who was the only one close to him and updated Austin the status of his businesses? Austin told him about the world behind the bars and asked Franklin to make him part of few more charities, few more random acts of kindness by increasing charities and donations. Franklin did everything Austin asked him but one day it went too far. Austin asked Franklin to sell all his businesses and to donate all the money to charities and for wellbeing of the people. Franklin denied. This was a rushed decision. By selling all the business he would put many people out of job which would be exactly opposite of "Act of Kindness".

Austin didn't want to be part of anything outside, especially his business which was built on the pillars of lies and deceit and the money earned from it was cursed. Franklin denied multiple times and so Austin took a drastic step. He called in his lawyer and drafted and sale deed in favour of Franklin. He gave all his business to Franklin who was already handling it and now owned it legally. Once the papers were signed and the deal was done, Austin felt a huge burden coming off his shoulders and he devoted his remaining life to God.

Looking at his good behaviour Austin was released in four years. All thanks again to Franklin who appealed in court and won with the appeal with help of some expensive lawyers.

Once Austin was out of jail, Franklin took him in. When they reached Franklin's home, Austin was surprised to know Franklin had married. He kept his marriage a secret and wanted to surprise Austin. The closer Franklin tried to get to Austin, the farther Austin felt like going. Austin didn't want any part of it. He then visited his mansion to relive his memories.

Franklin was aware of it and had it cleaned and renovated for Austin.

Franklin intended in slowly giving Austin his life and his business back. Inspite of his name on the company's legal documents, Franklin never considered himself the owner. This empire was built by Austin, and he was the rightful owner of it.

First, Franklin gave Austin his house back and discussed business with him regularly. Austin realized what Franklin was up to, but his mind was set. He didn't want to be part of anything that reminded him of his previous life. Then one night without any clue Austin took off. He left this place to never comeback.

Next day when Franklin reached Austin's house it was empty. Franklin searched all the places he knew and even logged a compliant with the cops, but nothing worked. Austin was smart enough to be able to hide away from the cops and specially Franklin who had put in efforts to find Austin. Mr Goel was still stationed in Goa and as he was aware of Austin's life, so he investigated this case personally.

Months passed but Austin wasn't seen in Goa. None of the CCTV cameras nor any person had seen him. He was back into 'Ghost mode' like was in his earlier days as Godless. The cops suspected he was out of Goa and looking for him was waste of time and efforts.

Earlier in his life Austin ran away from his brother to start a new life and same thing repeated. This time Austin ran away from Franklin to start a new life.

It was more than three years now since Austin ran away from Franklin who had now given up the search but still remembered him. With all the notes that Franklin had on Austin's life since day one, he did something he never thought he could do in his life. He wrote a book and dedicated it to Austin. He captured all the details that he observed since he was with Austin, the life that Kalyan narrated about Austin and about Godless. It was still a secret how he knew that Austin was Godless. Franklin captured almost everything that he could remember and made Austin the Hero of his story. This is what Sara had told Austin one day and it came true, but she had nothing to do with the book.

This book on Austin's life became one of the best sellers in India. Becoming an Author was never in the cards, but he wanted people to know about Austin's life. An incredible journey of ups and downs, rights and wrongs and love and hate. Austin's life had everything which made it an excellent book. This book was a success and later adopted by many filmmakers. Franklin became famous and was invited to many places for book signings. This diluted importance of Austin and Franklin had almost forgotten him. But he always missed the connection between them and just when Franklin turned over the page, Austin walked into his life.

It happened when Franklin was invited to Chennai for a book signing. Franklins' photos were up on hoardings all over Chennai which caught Austin's attention while he was travelling in a bus. Austin was hiding in Chennai. Franklin never would have guessed it in million years. They never did any business here and never spoke about Chennai, maybe that's why Austin chose this location. He finally took Kalyan's advice to move out of Goa.

Austin wasn't into books but was proud of Franklins achievement. He knew this was his story that Franklin authored in the book. He didn't care for it but was willing to see Franklin in person and so he decided to go visit him at the book signings…in disguise.

On the day of the book signing Franklin arrived at the hall at eleven sharp and there were at least fifty to seventy people in the line. It wasn't a huge turnout but among them was Austin wearing a fake beard, dark glasses, and a turban.

One by one the fans entered in, and Franklin signed their copy of the book. Some even took photos with Franklin. He was a celebrity now. When Austin entered the hall, the security asked him to take his glasses off. He then approached Franklin and handed him the book.

"To whom do i sign it for" asked Franklin looking at Austin.

"To life" replied Austin.

Franklin didn't recognize him instantly but as Austin walked away, Franklin suspected he had seen those eyes. He was close enough to Austin to remember those eyes and missed him too much that his senses lit up when Austin stood close to him. Franklin still had an hour left before the official time for the book signings was up and so he asked one of his assistants to follow Austin.

The assistant came back to the hotel after six hours with the details of the location where Austin got down from the bus. He couldn't get the name or any other details.

Franklin had a flight to catch in the night, but he still decided to pursue his suspicion and visit this address. He sat in his rented car and drove to this place. It was dark and this place was at the other end of Chennai bordering the 'Bay of Bengal'. He was guided by the GPS.

He reached the location at nine in the night. This was actually the end of road, and few steps ahead would take you to the seashore. This looked like a very small village and there were no lights on the road nor were there any numbers on the houses. With nobody around, asking for guidance was impossible. Franklin was frustrated after a long drive but didn't give up. He had now already missed his flight and so decided to knock on each door. He asked about Austin to the people who opened the door, but nobody understood Franklin who didn't speak Tamil. After tiring thirty minutes he reached a house which was different from the houses here and so he chose to peek in instead of knocking on the door. It was Franklins sixth sense that compelled him to peek in. Slowly, without making any noise moved towards the house and peeked in from the window. He was delighted to see Austin and he just kept watching him.

This reminded Franklin of the first night when he peeked into Austin's house. This was his second time doing the same thing. He was happy to see good old Austin on the couch as always watching football on the weekends.

Franklin thought of knocking on the door and letting Austin know that he had come for him. He had come to take him back to where he belonged. To give back the empire Austin created and owned. Franklin was always loyal to Austin, but these past years brought them closer. Austin always said Franklin was his brother from another mother.

Franklin thought Austin was all alone, and he couldn't watch him in this misery. Then just as he was about to knock on the window came in a woman with food. Franklin couldn't see the women's face as she was facing Austin but for a moment Franklin felt good assuming Austin started another life. Franklin calmed but then freaked out when he saw this lady's face... It was Sara.

Instantly a shiver passed through Franklins body, and he ran away from the window and sat in his car. This was too much to take in and he needed a breather to gather his thoughts. He was surprised to see Austin here but was more shocked to Sara. She left him long before Austin was arrested and the revealing of the "Hitman" that grandpa was. How was this even possible that they both were staying together.

On the other hand, Franklin was extremely happy that Sara and Austin were united. They were meant to be, and he was dying to meet them but wasn't sure that they both felt the same, after all they choose to hide away from him and their previous life.

As he sat in the car thinking about it there was a knock on the car's window. Franklin looked up and it was Austin and Sara. He looked at them and opened the door, but Austin closed it. Then Sara and Austin, both got in the backseat of the car.

"You have a habit of peeking in my home huh. But I caught you twice doing that" said Austin and added "How does it feel to be at the top".

This was a strange question given the circumstances. At first Franklin thought Austin might ask about how he found him and what was happening in Goa, but he asked something unrelated to the situation.

"I don't think I am at the top. I am doing good but definitely not at the top" replied Franklin.

"Nonsense. You own hotels and business and now are a famous writer. If this is not being at the top than what is," said Austin.

"Can I turnaround, it's really weird to talk to the steering wheel" asked Franklin.

"Okay" Replied Sara.

"First of all, I don't consider myself at the top as I never earned any of it. I mean I manage the business you once built with your hard work and intelligence, and I wrote a book that is based on your life. Nothing in it is mine." And added, "How are you guys and if we are done with this nonsense jibber jabber, do you mind telling me what the hell is going on. You couldn't stay away from the beach either huh".

"Why did you come here? you shouldn't be here. Why are you here?" asked Sara.

"I don't know if you guys consider me a family, but I surely do. I understand that you wanted to stay away from the life in Goa but why would you abandon me? After everything that we've been through?" asked Franklin desperately seeking answers.

"I made two mistakes when I got out of the drug business. First one was not leaving Goa as Kalyan had suggested and second one was not taking care of Romeo when i sensed he was trouble for me. I was blinded by the money and the power and look what I got in return. When I came to Goa, I was clueless on what was going to happen. I didn't plan things to go this way. It just happened and that flow of things gave me money, gave me fame but took away my family and trust me, money is nothing when you don't have a family. I have a family now and I wouldn't put it at risk again. There are still many people in Goa trying to get back at me," said Austin.

When Austin said a "Family" he hinted that Sara was pregnant, but Franklin didn't pick it.

"Yes, you are right, and I agree. I will ensure nobody knows. But well stay in touch" replied Franklin and both Sara and Austin looked at each other. Sara nodded her head 'yes 'and they all agreed.

The Austin asked, "how did you knew that I was Godless and who told you about my time in the drug business. That's right I read your book. You did a good job making me a hero. Sara also had this idea of writing a book on my story. But I am glad that you came out with it and it's a success"

"The evidence that was left with the cops, I managed to get my hands on them and was surprised when I learned that you were Godless. The book was just the notes that I maintained since day one. Godless was a hero to many and he had to be the hero in my book too" replied Franklin and added, "Now tell me the truth. Tell me when and how did you guys come here" asked Franklin.

"The death of Kalyan and Franky was too much for me and that's when I decided I wasn't going to lose Sara. I told her everything about my past and that scared her. She didn't want any part of it, but she loved me, and our love pulled her in this mess. She saw how I was a changed man since she came into my life and gave me another chance at life. So, we made up a plan to get out of this chaos, stay away from the danger and live our life in peace. I knew that someone was sabotaging my life and not knowing who that person was the scariest part. I had already sensed that after the murder of Kalyan and Franky that Devil of death will come for Sara and when she received the envelope, it was time for her to go missing. She collected all the cash that we had around this house and our house in Panvel and went in search of a location where nobody from our previous life would ever find us. After she escaped, I was alone at home and this loneliness was perfect for me to fake a miserable life. With Kalyan and my brother dead, attack on my life and then Sara going away, all these actually helped me in court, and you know how it went. Anyways, suddenly the cops came to my house and the next day they found Grandpa. It all happened so fast that I couldn't think and got trapped in jail. That wasn't it, during the first few months in jail, I couldn't reach Sara. She wasn't aware that I was in jail. After few months she got to know that I was arrested and then she reached out to me. I thought she must have left me or maybe something happened to her. It was too much of pain and few times I tried to kill myself. But then out of nowhere Sara was there waiting for me in the meeting room and that's when we planned the rest of our lives. Far from everyone and everything. We have a good thing going here, do not mess it up" said Austin. Not all of this was true though, Austin never told Franklin that Sara knew everything all the way.

"Don't worry I'll leave you at it, but we'll meet again. I will be back, and you let me know if you need anything" said Franklin and he left with a promise to be back.

He was extremely happy to see both of them, but they didn't look that happy and Franklin sensed it. Franklin went back to Goa and came back to meet them after ten days. But Franklin's excitement was ruined when he found the house was empty. None of the neighbours knew anything about them. One neighbour though recognized him as Mr Philip Gonsalves. It seemed the latest name Austin went by.

Franklin knew, if Austin wanted to stay hidden nobody would be able to find him. Saddened by the event he turned around and went back. This time he was really hurt and decided he wasn't going to waste time on trying to find Austin. He set his mind on closing his doors for Austin and going on with his life. That was the end of it. Franklin never met him, or Sara again is his life.

Few days later Franklin became a dad and they moved to Austin's house which was an excellent place to bring up a kid. He was a legitimate businessman and even more successful with nothing to hide. He was married to lovely girl and had the cutest baby girl.

One evening Franklin was telling his wife the adventurous story of Austin. A man who changed his name thrice to deal with different phases of his life and he remembered Chris. In all this chaos, Chris was the victim. He was still away at a foster home and post discussing with his wife Franklin decided to bring him home to stay with them.

Next morning, he went to the foster care alongwith his wife and enquired about Chris. At first the warden denied sharing any information but then post receiving a donation from Franklin he mentioned that Chris was taken away by a family few months ago. Franklin asked him the details of the family who adopted Chris and again the warden kept mum. Franklin then added another zero to the earlier donation and the warden digged out the details of the family who has sheltered Chris. When the warden showed the computer screen to Franklin, he saw only the fathers name and it shocked him. Chris was adopted by Mr. Philip Gonsalves.

www.ingramcontent.com/pod-product-compliance
Lightning Source LLC
LaVergne TN
LVHW041702060526
838201LV00043B/530